BREAK CONTACT

by

Shawn Michael

Revised November 2019

CHAPTER 1

Mission Reviled

There is a lot of activity around the UN base, soldiers coming and going on foot and in trucks. There are three men standing at the base of a communications tower running cabling and a women working on a laptop.

Up in the tower is a forth man who is adjusting dishes and antennas. As certain trucks pass by, the man on the tower clicks on a hidden microphone. "Truck number 0487 and 8287." At the bottom the woman hears the information and puts the information in her work sheet in a code, "Copy." She says quietly.

Captain Mihailov is standing inside one of the tents across from the telecom tower that the technicians are working on. Capt. Mihaiov calls out, "Senior Sgt Vladimir." Moments later Sr. Sgt. Vladimir enters the tent. "Ivan they are up to something, I don't know what it is yet. Take five men and arrest them." Says Capt. Mihailov. Sgt.

Vladimir nods in acknowledgement of his orders; he turns and exits the tent.

Moments later Sgt. Vladimir and five other UN soldiers have surrounded the telecom workers with their weapons at the ready. "Down on your knees, hands behind your heads." Sgt. Vladimir points to the man in the tower. "You, you need to come down NOW! You are all under arrest." States Sgt. Vladimir. The four on the ground comply and the fifth man starts climbing down and he is angry. "What the hell is going on, we have work to do. We are under cont…." There is a gunshot that takes everyone by surprise and the telecom worker falls to the ground.

"Take them all to the holding facility." Says Sgt. Vladimir. The men start gathering up the four telecom workers and moving them to a covered truck. "I said all of them, unless one of you want to take the dead man's place." Commands Sgt. Vladimir. They rush to get the body loaded into the truck. They load up into the truck and it drives off.

* * * * * * * * * * * * * * * *

Mac woke to the ringing of his phone. It took a moment for him to surface from a deep sleep and answer.

"They have requested your EEA, if you accept it, we move in an hour," Don said flatly, then hung up. Mac looked at the clock, 0200 hours.

Mac lay next to Sandy, feeling her warmth, not wanting to move.

Pondering where are we heading this time?

As Mac got out of bed, Sandy rolled over, "What are you doing up so late?"

"I have to go to work," he said walking into the bathroom.

Sandy heard the shower and saw the steam begin to fill the bathroom they shared. She sat up in bed and stretched the sleep from her limbs, pushing sleep out of her lithe body.

"Why do you get these mysterious calls in the middle of the night and head off to." Sandy pauses "Wait, I thought your contract was over." she stated.

Mac stood in the hot stream of water. Shook his head and shrugged his shoulders. He could hear the frustration in her voice; he knew where this was going.

Mac could see her through the foggy glass shower door: arms crossed, her posture inviting an explanation or an excuse. It was up to him, and he was a mixture of excitement and auto pilot.

"Look, I told you when we got together, my job is complicated and I am on call twenty-four/seven. You know I work for CPS, (Corporate Protective Services) as a Security Consultant. And yes my contract was up a week ago, but for thirty days CPS can request what is called an EEA, {Emergency Extension Agreement), it's a request to extend a consultant on terminal leave through an emergency situation. I can decline which ends all commitment to CPS. But if I accept they will pay me half of my yearly salary for one mission. That's one hundred thousand dollars for a couple of days work and we could put that toward our future. When I get back, if you still want to know, I promise I will tell you exactly what I do but I don't have the time to do this now."

"You've never told me what you do! I have asked you. I've felt your scars. I've sensed the pain in your heart. I want to help you carry their weight. But, you shut me out. Are you some kinda spy, or a Mafia hit man?"

Both thought Mac. He turned off the water, opened the door. Sandy handed him a towel without uttering another word. His turn.

"No, I'm not a spy or a hit man. My work is . . . . I help people, it's what I do. I don't talk about it, I just--"

"Whatever." Sandy walked passed him into the bedroom. She stopped herself from reaching out to touch him. She wanted to make him tell her, hold her, trust her but, she was protecting herself. Too many questions. She wanted answers.

* * * * * * * * * * * * * * *

Mac sits on the bed beside Sandy. He knows what he wants to do, and he knows what he has to do. "You know I'm at a point where I'm questioning what I do. If I or the team even make a difference anymore. But unfortunately there is not much else I'm qualified to do. Even if I could I would never go back to the Corps after their betrayal, I sure the hell don't want to wear a badge anymore, especially when you trust the criminals more than your bosses. I can't spend every day playing golf and I sure can't sit around the house all day playing EVE on the computer. You know I have been contemplating what direction my, our future is going to take. I was supposed to have thirty days to decide. We can decide if I continue with it or I do something else, but I don't have the time to do this now." Not enough he thought to himself.

Mac dressed with his back to her. Sandy isn't moving, her eyes glow in the light. Mac reiterates, "Sandy I'm serious, if you're still here when I get back, we will talk about what I do."

Sandy slowly moves from the bed, puts her arms around him from behind and kisses his shoulder, pressing her cheek against him. She will not give up on him, she has secrets, too. A past.

Mac slowly turns around, puts his arms around her, and feels her warmth. He slides his hand up her back into the tangle of red hair and looks into her eyes. Those limpid pools of blue bordered by emerald green. He kissed her, the sweet kiss of caring. She bit his lower lip, "Good, I'd hate to cut you off till you told me."

Sandy breaks the embrace; jumps back into bed and give Mac an inviting picture of her. She is in profile, the swell of her breasts, her slender figure an invitation he cannot accept. She smiles her smile and winks.

"Damn, that is just wrong," he says somewhere between desire and duty, audible torture, "Everything I do, I do for us, this house, our cars, life isn't cheap."

Mac leans forward and kisses her cheek, smells her crazy curls. He moves his hand along her side until his palm rests on her tush, his fingers feel the heat coming from the cleft of her buttocks. He cannot, will not. His hand retraces its steps as he stands up. One last whiff of her beauty and want.

He turns off the bathroom light. He's got to go.

Is this the last time he will see her? He turns to her, "Sandy, I love you."

* * * * * * * * * * * * * * *

Walking down the hall Mac is full of emotions. He must ready his gear and put Sandy out of his mind, for now.

In the basement, he releases a catch on the back wall and pushes the wall open to reveal a hidden room. The room is 14' X 14', the size of a bedroom. Shelves line the side walls; the end of the room houses a large door gun safe. Mac grabs an olive drab flight bag, and a black nylon rifle bag. He opens the biometric gun safe and surveys his personal armory. Mac surveys his choices. He takes a moment to take them all in. He selects a Stoner 63A automatic rifle. He smiled, there are only a handful left in existence. Mac acquired it through his military contacts. This is his Holy Grail of weapons. Mac automatically performs a safety check and places it in the bag. He also takes his tried and true Glock 19, 9mm. Mac checks the flight bags to make sure it is good to go, then takes 10, 200 round belt-fed ammo boxes and puts them in the bag. The room secured, Mac is ready.

In the garage, he walks toward his baby, a custom built 2013, burnt orange, Dodge Challenger SRT8 convertible. The top is down and he tosses his gear in the back seat. He opens the garage doors, settles behind the wheel and fires it up. The sound of the horses oozes from it. He backs it out and heads down the street as the garage door closes. Sandy and his life with her grows smaller, he is looking straight ahead.

* * * * * * * * * * * * * * *

It took Mac thirty minutes to get to the private airport. Mac stops at the security gate. The Guard opens the window to the booth and extends his left arm with a clenched fist as a greeting. Mac shakes his head, ignoring the fist bump, and hands the guard his ID. Irritated by the snub, the guard takes Mac's Corporate Protective Services (CPS) ID Card. The guard checks it against his list of authorized personnel and hands it back. The guard starts to say something to Mac.

"You know I was a Marine, how about,"

but is cut short.

"Sorry Henwood, you just don't have what we are looking for. Try a University or something." states Mac as he drives off.

When he got there Don and Dennis where waiting next to the all black Bombardier BD-700 jet.

Mac parked the challenger. As he gets out he waved at Don and Dennis. Mac smiles and grabs his weapons bag. He is about to rock their worlds. He takes the Stoner out of the bag, opens the bolt, gun clear. He looks up and sees their wide, envious faces.

Dennis exclaims, "NO WAY! You got it, you lucky SOB!"

Don chuckles and pushes Dennis; he knows how much Dennis wants that rifle. Mac hands the Stoner to Dennis. Mac knows Dennis is elated.

"Dude, I can't believe it." Dennis only has eyes for the Stoner, "Shiiiiit," he says lovingly.

"Yeah, it took some doing cash and favors," Mac told them.

"Don, I hope it's okay, it's all I brought."

"No problem. It will give us a small advantage," Don says with a knowing smile.

In the meantime, Dennis is walking off with the Stoner, Mac grabs him and the Stoner, "If you're good, I'll let you give it a test drive."

"You bet your ass you will." Dennis is beaming.

Mac grabs his gear, secures the car and they walk toward the plane.

"So, where to this time boys?" Mac asks.

"Don't know yet," says Dennis, "we're waiting on the package, then we have to pick up the brothers. Once we are in the air again we can open it."

Moments after Mac loaded his gear, a dark van pulls up. The passenger door and the side van door opens. A man in a suit exits from the passenger door and a man dressed in fatigues from the side door. The Suit and Dennis walk towards each other and shake hands. He hands Dennis a manila envelope. They exchange words, and as far as Mac can see, it wasn't all pleasantries. Don and Mac looked at each other and at the man standing next to the van. The Suit walked away from

Dennis and over to the man at the van, they shook hands and exchanged words.

Dennis approached Don and Mac, "They have added a member to our team, it's not open for discussion or debate, understood!"

Don starts to say something, but is cut off by Dennis, "What part of 'Not Open for Discussion' didn't you understand?" Dennis and the new guy walk past Don and Mac. They all board the plane.

Mac opened the cockpit door, "Hello girls, guess we are off for more fun and adventure." he says to Jack and Tim, the pilot and copilot. Mac steps into the cabin and extends his hand. Jack and Tim have taken them on more missions than any of the other CPS pilots. Mac has known both of them for about four years now. Tim and Mac do things outside of work and Mac calls him McDaddy, as his last name is McDermitt. They play golf, have dinner at each other's homes, he knows his wife and two daughters. Mac considers him a friend.

Tim and Jack both shake Mac's hand. Tim, "Well, whatever it is I wish you guys the best of luck. All I know is you are the best that we have." Jack laughs, "Shit we are in trouble." We laugh and Mac heads out of the cockpit. Mac passes Dennis in the hallway.

Dennis lets the pilots know they are good to go, "The first leg of the flight should take about an hour to get to our first destination." Once airborne, Dennis introduced the new guy,

"This is Steve, he will be joining our Team and will have the designation of Six, he is a former member of the Rangers and a combat vet," Dennis points to Don, "This is Don his designation is Two, as in my second-in-command."

"This is Mac, his designation is Three, you will meet the other two team members at our next stop."

Dennis takes Steve to the other end of the plane for a private conversation. As they fly into the night, Don and Mac spent the next hour catching up. Mac has known Dennis and Don for twenty years. All three used to be police officers and have some type of military training or Emergency Response Training background. They have worked together indirectly for CPS in one capacity or another for about five years off and on, on different projects before they became a

Team Ten years ago. Steve's presence has placed some questions as to the readiness of the team.

Dennis takes a break from interrogating Steve and walked up to Don and Mac who are talking and he sits down.

"What are you two plotting, a coup?" asks Dennis. Both Don and Mac laugh. "I'm glad you have a minute I kinda need to talk to you both." Says Mac. "I apologize for not talking to you earlier about this, but as you both know I'm on my terminal leave, I'm frustrated over something Sandy said and she didn't know how close she really was to the truth. It's not like when we started out; I don't feel like I'm helping anyone anymore, it feels like all I'm doing is someone else's dirty work. Are we just hired guns?" Don leans forward in his seat. "I know it seems like it, but we just do what is asked of us. It's not always gonna be saving lives and winning the girl."

Dennis laughs. "You already got the girl Mac, and saving the day isn't always what it's cut out to be. It's not like in the movies, not everyone comes home." "Yeah I know that, I guess I want to be more than someone else's hired gun." States Mac. Dennis sighs. "We are more than that Mac. We help those who cannot or are unable to help themselves. Yes, we have been hired guns, but I think overall we are much more than that."

They didn't realize they were landing until they feel the plane touchdown.

"We can talk more about this later. Smith has tasked me with talking you into staying." Says Dennis.

* * * * * * * * * * * * * * *

They land at another private airport. Once the plane comes to a stop Don opens the hatch and they exit the plane to stretch their legs and spend some time talking and getting to know Steve while they wait on the arrival of 'the brothers.'

Mac has worked with the brothers twice before, first on an operation into Vietnam and a training exercise with the Air Force Security Force. The brothers, John and Mark, are good old southern boys. John is the older of the two; he stands about six feet tall and around one hundred and eighty pounds with short brown hair. The younger brother, Mark, stands about five foot ten inches, and matches John at one hundred and eighty pounds with short sandy blonde hair.

It was about ten minutes before they saw headlights heading their way. The truck they were driving pulled up and the doors opened and out came the brothers. Greetings were exchanged; introductions to the new guy, pats on the backs and everyone loaded their gear on the plane. Airborne again.

Once in the air, Dennis opened the sealed envelope. He takes out documents, photographs, maps and empty envelopes. As he hands out envelopes to everyone, "You all know the routine." Dennis looks to Steve, "All your personal effects." As everyone is putting their belongings away, Dennis begins briefing us on our mission:

"Approximately twenty-four hours ago, five members of a private telecommunications company were working in Georgia when they were taken hostage by an unidentified group. Our mission is to go in, get them out with as little collateral damage as possible. Since the US government won't officially get involved in recovery operations for private companies we have been empowered to do just that. With CPS's connections in the FBI, CIA and State Department, we have been able to get some satellite time from the area and they have been able to put together a pretty good idea where the hostages are located.

"At this time, we don't have any Intel on how many hostiles, what they want, if they are military or some extremist group. CPS hopes to be able to provide that information as it becomes available."

John asked, "Who are the five people, who do they work for and why are they there in the first place?"

Dennis, with his attempt to be serious, said "It's need to know."

Everyone but Steve replies, "We know, we know…we don't need to know."

Mac chimes in, "But, for the record, these things are always more complicated when you say that."

Dennis continued the briefing, "We will be inserted by chopper close to the Turkey/Georgia border, travel by foot into Georgia, hopefully undetected to a building that is presumed to be heavily guarded. We will enter the building undetected, recover the hostages and return to the designated extraction point back in Turkey." They all chuckle as they know damn well that's never what happens.

They spent the next few hours going over the satellite photos and what Intel they had. Each member added what information they had of the area. Eventually, they all got some much needed sleep. They knew they would need to be well rested and sharp on the upcoming op. Mac gets up and pulls Dennis aside. "You know there is more to this than we are being told, too much Intel in twenty four hours. I don't like it." Before Dennis can respond Mac walks away.

Mac doesn't know about the others, but it was hard to sleep with the anticipation of the operation ahead of them, and his promise to Sandy. Mac slipped in and out of a restless sleep visualizing all the possible variables. Dennis was awake already and looking over the brief and photos again, but the others were still sleeping. Mac grabbed a pad of paper and a pen and started writing:

Sandy,

If you get this in the mail or is hand delivered things didn't go well and I won't be able to answer your questions in person.

I know I haven't been overly forthcoming about my work, but there is a reason for that. The work I do is considered by some people to be immoral or illegal.

What I do, I do to help people. This is very hard for me, because I don't want you to think less of me. I know I'm stalling, and that is why I am writing this letter because you deserve to know the truth. You will have questions and I will answer them as best I can. As you know I used to be a Cop, before that I spent some time in the Marine Corps before I was medically retired.

I have been trained in the art of soldiering. About fifteen years ago I went to work for CPS, Inc., (Corporate Protective Services, Inc.) For lack of a better term, I am a consultant. I protect people, consult on how to protect people, do investigative work, things like that. But, the main job description would be asset recovery. I know you are asking what an asset is. Well we recover people, people who have been kidnapped or taken against their will. We go to places that the Government won't go, or can't go. We actually do work off the books for the Government.

What it all comes down to is that I am a corporate hired gun, a mercenary, or any number of names you can come up with. What I do is to help people, to save people whose lives are in peril and no one else can help them. I know the next question that you are thinking about. The answer is yes, but only to protect or save lives. Only people who are trying to hurt or kill others or to kill me, it needs to be clear, I am not an assassin.

Well that is what I do; I hope you understand why I have not been more forthcoming. I have to close now as I am about to go to work.

But I want you to know I love you.

Mac

Mac felt the landing gear go down as he put the letter in an envelope. Mac addressed the envelope to Sandy and put the letter in his pocket. The guys were all awake but Mac hadn't noticed while he was writing. The plane came to a stop in a large hanger and the hatch opened. As Mac headed to the door, Tim comes out from the cockpit. Mac stops Tim and hands him the letter. He looked Tim straight in the eyes. "We both know the policy, but do me a favor buddy. Hang onto this for me and mail this once you get back to the states if anything goes wrong?"

Tim pats Mac's shoulder, "You will be fine Mac, but you have my word."

CHAPTER 2

First Contact

Jack and Tim gather up their gear also and exit the jet. They meet with a man, dressed in fatigues, before they make their way to a Huey located on the other side of the hanger. Once they get there, they unpack their gear and start inspecting the helicopter, and doing its preflight check.

The team off loads the gear and unpack it. They spend the next couple of hours doing equipment and weapons checks. Everyone's gear and weapons are good to go. They go over their assignments and designations, Dennis is (1) Team Leader, Don is (2), second lead, our sniper. Mac is (3), weapons specialist/demolitions man. John is (4), he carries the SAW. Mark is (5), our combat medic and communication specialist, Steve is (6), a weapons specialist.

It's still daylight out as they head toward the Huey. Tim, standing there with his foot up on the floor plate and leaning on his thigh, is approached by Mac, "Just make sure your there to get us out okay?"

Tim smiled, "You think I'd let you have all the fun."

They load up the gear and board the Huey. There are four crew members: Tim, the pilot; Jack, the copilot, and two door gunners manning the M60's. The rotors start spinning up and the chopper heads to the East flying low to avoid detection.

* * * * * * * * * * * * * * *

After three hours flight in the air, it's still daylight as Tim clicks his mic, "The LZ is in sight." Dennis looks at Tim and gives him a thumbs up. Dennis taps each of the team members to get their attention. Once Dennis has their attention, "Lock and load gentlemen, it's game time."

The Huey descends and inserts the team into a small clearing. Mac is the last one to exit the chopper as the packs and weapons are off loaded. As Mac steps onto the skid he takes a small pack from his rucksack and slides it under Tim's seat. Mac pats him on the shoulder and gives him the thumbs up, Tim returns the gesture. As Mac joins the rest of the team that has gathered in the tree line watching the Huey fade off into the horizon. Once the sound of the blades has dissipated the team spends about thirty minutes surveying the area for any activity or movement.

They conduct another check of their gear, and set off into the country side. It has been dark for about eight hours and they have walked till their legs screamed for rest. They dropped their packs and took turns keeping watch as the others slept. Mac kept first watch. After about an hour, Mac woke John for the next watch.

Mac closed his eyes and fell asleep, he dreamed of days past, time he spent with his friends, family, parents, siblings, his son … and a woman who could, should, be his wife.

Mac was jolted out of his dream by a hand being placed over his mouth and being shaken … it was barely light out, his eyes looked into Don eyes and then Mac followed his eyes as he looked into the trees … It took a few seconds, but then he saw what Don was looking at. A small patrol of armed men, ten in total. Mac slowly picked up the Stoner and prepared for the worst … Mac noticed that Dennis had woken the brothers and they were also preparing their weapons as Don woke Steve and John.

The group of men slowly moved off in the opposite direction, they seemed unaware of the team's position. The insertion was as good as it gets.

Once the group was out of sight, they gathered up our gear. Don and Mac placed several claymores on the ground and in the trees, with trip wires attached to them to cover them if the group decided to return. To deter the local wildlife, they relieved themselves around the area. A human wouldn't be able to detect the scent, but the animals would. Once the mines were in place, we slowly moved in the opposite direction.

The team walked for about three hours, when Don, on point, came to a break in the cover he hesitated. There was an opening with a dirt road leading to a bridge. Don signaled for Mac to cover right and Dennis to cover left. As Don moved out of cover Dennis broke to the left to cover the road and Mac broke to the right. It was clear at first, then Mac saw a man stand up, holding an AK-47. As the weapon began to rise Mac hollered, "Contact right." His Stoner was bearing down on the man's torso as Mac moved toward the soldier.

His weapon was seated in his shoulder, his sights on the man's chest. Mac could see the muzzle flash from the AK-47, as he squeezed his own trigger. The distinctive sound of the AK stopped as the man took six rounds in the chest and fell to the ground.

Mac kept his weapon at the ready as he approached. The rest of the team created a perimeter and secured the area as Mac kneeled next to him and checked for a pulse. The soldier was dead.

Each member of the team relayed no other visible contacts and no injuries. Don pats Mac on the shoulder and said, "If we only gave purple hearts." He lifted Mac's left arm and showed him that he had taken a round.

Mac never felt the round until he saw the wound. "Okay, now that hurts, you didn't have to show me," as he punched Don in the shoulder.

Don laughs, "Mark can you clean and wrap that for Mr. Whiny."

Steve kept watch as Dennis and John gathered up the man's body and cleaned up the area where the body was while Mark patched

Mac up. They carried the body off and left it in the brush as they continued toward the objective. They all knew that the stakes just got higher.

At midday, the team was moving through the brush as Don gave the signal to hold position. The team held their positions and scanned the area ahead of them. Don motioned that there was a patrol inbound. He instructed them to setup for an ambush. They spread out into an "L" formation with Don on top, then John, Dennis and Steve. Mark and Mac were in the swing arm position. The patrol was on course straight into the ambush.

As they closed, the team's weapons were trained on them, fingers on triggers. Mac could see the look of surprise, the look of horror as the lead man saw Don and the weapon pointed at him. The soldier's eyes were the size of baseballs as he realized what was about to happen. The man's mouth opened but no sound came. The man's weapon was in his hands at his waist. He turned his head to look at the rest of his patrol, his weapon rising as he looked back at Don. The last thing he would ever see was the muzzle flash of Don's M-4. That was our signal to open up.

Bullets ripped through their flesh. The first four men in the patrol dropped before they could even raise their weapons. The remaining six men began to fire back and headed for whatever cover they could find.

Don emptied his magazine, hollered "break contact right. Moving," and withdrawing to the back of the team. As he passed John he slapped him on the shoulder signaling John was now point. Don moved past Mac and Mark and continuing right, moving into the brush.

John did the same, his M-60 empty, leaving Dennis as point. The same went for Dennis, Steve, then Mac and finally Mark. The team had broken contact and set up a new ambush fifty yards to the right of the initial point of contact.

Mac scanned the area in front of him looking for the patrol not knowing if they could or would pursue.

The hostile patrol wasn't very discreet in their pursuit; they must not have been professional soldiers, they rushed into another blaze of automatic fire. Three M-4's, an AK, a SAW and a Stoner 63A throwing a wall of hot lead at the approaching patrol. They stopped in their tracks as their bodies fell to the ground. The team broke contact and moved away from the objective to keep further patrols guessing.

CHAPTER 3

Objective

It was dark by the time they reached the main objective. The moon was full and visibility dangerous for the team. Mac viewed the large structure ahead through his night vision binoculars. He could see multiple silhouettes in and around the building. Mac scanned the ground between their position and the building. It was a very large clearing, high grass, trees-- no real cover to use. They were three hundred yards from the target. The building was a faded white wash, four stories high with part of the first level below ground. The building was about three hundred feet long, with windows about every five feet on every floor. The windows were either boarded up or broken out, and no light was visible.

Dennis took out a monocular and started to scan the building.

"I have multiple heat signatures on the top two floors, top floor has the smaller number of people and the third floor has the most. There are some scattered heat sigs on the other two floors and some in the field between us. There are also four to six guards on the roof."

The team made a plan for approach and retreat: Don and Steve were to stay in the tree line to provide sniper and artillery support if needed. Dennis and Mark would head to the other side of the building, while John and Mac would take this side of the building and make entry.

Dennis could not be sure, but he believed the hostages were being held on the fourth floor. One room had a cluster of heat sigs and two heat sigs that were separate from them, as if guards. There were about ten to fifteen other heat sigs on the fourth floor. The third floor had too many to count and were spread out the length of the building. The Intel photos showed another building and water tower behind the large building.

It was about 0300 hours, when they stripped off any unnecessary gear, checked coms, and moved out of the tree line. The team used an old fence line to cover their approach. They were able to move a 100 yards under its cover before it ended.

Mac gave Don the night vision before Dennis, Mark, John and Mac began low crawling through the high grass. It took Mac about an hour before he reached the first guard. Dennis and Mark had further to go to the other side. Don watched through the night vision until most of the movement had died down. He guided them to the guards that were bedded down in the grass. Mac was within striking distance of the guard, his head was toward Mac and he was lying on his back, snoring softly.

Mac drew a knife from his harness; his left hand covered the sleeping man's mouth as Mac's right hand drove the blade up under his chin and into the man's brain, the body shook for a moment then went limp. Mac withdrew the blade and wiped it off on the dead man's clothes. Don advised Mac he should be clear. Mac continued to crawl toward the building.

Once John and Mac reached the building he contacted Don, "Two this is Four. Looking for entry."

"Four, this is Two. Clear."

John and Mac crawled along the base of the building looking for a window to gain entry. They found a window close to the south corner of the building. John slowly entered the window, it was dark, but the full moon helped illuminate the room. Not knowing how far down the floor was, John slowly withdrew his tactical light, he covered the light with his hand and pushed the button. He pointed the light inside the room and slowly removed his hand to shed some light. John could see the floor just four feet down. The floor was concrete; it had some debris on it but nothing that would make noise. John entered first. Once in he donned his night vision, and checked the floor and room for glass or trip wires. The room was clear and Mac followed him in and activated his night vision. Once into the room John notified Don they had made entry. Dennis advised that they were in position and looking to make entry.

John and Mac moved slowly to the room's door, they were in a crouched walk, their knees bent, heel to toe, short steps. The door was slightly ajar and John slowly opened it not making any noise. They entered the hallway. They knew nothing, but a wall was behind them as they moved toward the center of the building. Still moving slowly, heel to toe, short steps. John was on the left side of the hallway Mac had the right. Their weapons at the ready.

They reached a set of stairs that was in the central area in the building. They visually checked for trip wires and booby traps, but so far so good. The other end of the hallway was dark and they couldn't see anything moving. Slowly they moved up the stairs to the second floor, Don advised that there were no heat sigs and they should be clear to proceed up the stairs.

****

Dennis and Mark had reached what they believed to be the front of the building. Dennis activated his mic and advised they had multiple guards standing outside at the entrance doors and would not be able to enter without a fire fight. Dennis and Mark held their position. It would be up to the Mac and John to enter.

****

As Mac and John reached the third floor they could hear movement off in the wings.

Don's voice came across Mac's ear piece, "Again advising that no one was moving on the third floor. There was movement on the fourth." They slowly continued to the top of the stairs on the fourth floor. They could hear movement and talking again. Some form of Russian or Bosnian. John covered the north end of the building and Mac had the south. They believed the hostages were in the south wing and Mac slowly moved down the hallway. Mac was about halfway down the hall when the mic went off, "Movement from third headed up," is all Don got out as the cracking of gun fire broke the silence of the night. Mac looked back toward John and saw him lunge forward and hit the floor. Mac could see lights being turned on, lanterns being fired up to provide light to see what was going on. Mac shed his night vision; it took a moment for his eyes to adjust.

* * * * * * * * * * * * * * * *

Dennis and Mark opened up on the guards at the door eliminating them before they had time to raise a weapon. Mark and Dennis stayed behind cover waiting for anyone to exit the building.

Don and Steve reached out and took care of the guards on the roof as they tried to figure out what had happened. Don could see lights and activity from the other building and warned that there was probably more hostile's incoming.

* * * * * * * * * * * * * * *

Mac turned around to see a man with an AK open a door and look down the hallway. Mac could hear yelling. All he could make out was something "AMERICANS!" Mac could hear gunfire and could see flashes from the room with the open door. Mac pulled the trigger, and released it, three or four rounds fired and the man fell back into the door dropping his weapon. Mac was taking fire from behind. Mac returned fire to the other end of the building as he approached the open door.

Mac hit the ground and made a low entry to find the person firing. The window or covering had been shot out and some light from the moon was slightly lighting the room. Mac could make out bodies on the floor by the window and a man standing over a body with an AK pointed at it.

"Drop the weapon or I will fire." Mac screamed out, in an angry and aggressive voice. The man looked to Mac, but the weapon never moved.

"You're American?" he exclaimed.

Mac had his weapon still trained on him, Mac stood up, and again Mac gave him an order. "Yes, now drop the weapon."

The man dropped the weapon and turned to the captives. Mac moved to check a body, he was dead. Mac picked up the weapon and walked over to the man, who was tending to the wounded captives. As Mac handed the man the AK he could see blood on his hands.

"Right now, I need your help, you obviously know how to use this." Mac told him.

The man smirked, "Well, you could say that."

Mac thought to himself...*Damn he's kinda cocky for just being saved.*

Mac took him to the door way and pointed back down the hallway.

"I need cover fire, I don't care if you hit anything, just don't shoot me!"

The man pointed the weapon down the hallway, "Not to worry, friend, I have some payback to get." He fires the weapon down the hallway, in controlled bursts.

Bullets were flying down the hallway and hitting all around the guards. Mac got low and headed back toward the stairs. He could see that John had moved himself off the stairs and had taken cover.

"Can you move?" asked Mac.

In a sarcastic, pissed off tone, John answered, "Oh, hell yes, took the main brunt in the vest, minor leg wound. I have been firing down the stairs to keep them there."

Mac grabbed the harness on the back of John's vest, "You shoot while I get us to cover." Mac handed him the Stoner and took off down the hallway.

Mac could see the man firing from the doorway providing cover, then he looked back and John was laying down cover with the M-4 in one hand, the Stoner in the other. Mac reached the doorway, slid into the door and dragged John inside. Mac told one man to go and check on his people. Mac got out his first aid kit and bandaged up Johns leg, then sent him over to check on the hostages. Mac returned to the man covering door.

"Two this is Three, advising on status, Four has minor, we have no, repeat, no exit at this time, very hostile, stand by for status."

"Three this is Two, clear will advise," stated Don.

"Two this is One, we are hot and withdrawing from this location. Unable to provide help current location, will provide support." said Dennis.

Dennis and Mark look at each other and they are off and running back toward the rally point.

* * * * * * * * * * * * * * * *

The gunfire was getting more intense from down the hallway. Mac could see the men advancing to the stairs for cover. Mac grabbed the dead guard's AK and dragged him into the room. Once he was inside Mac pulled the door toward him leaving a few inch opening to shoot out of. Mac searched the dead guard for ammunition and any other equipment they could use. The guard had three, thirty-round magazines on him and one mag in the rifle.

John got on the radio, "Two this is Four, be advised two of the five are dead, one is wounded in the shoulder and one is a female."

"Ah shit. Four this is One, photo ID dead, working on extraction."

John breaks out the camera and photographs the two dead men. John also checks the bodies for any identification. He notices on one of the dead bodies, one of the pant legs had been torn open and there was a fresh incision on the thigh and a dirty bandage had been pulled back. John didn't know what to make of it, but continued with the job of gathering their ID's.

"Hey John, you got any rope in your bags?" asks Mac.

"Yeah got rope, you got an idea?"

Mac tosses his rope to John, "Tie this off; we lower the three. Barricade the door, let the guys provide cover, we Australian out of here down the rope and head to the rally."

"Might work," says John.

"I need all the mags and grenades you have so I can keep them busy," Mac tells John.

John brings Mac the grenades and mags for the AK. John then moves to the window and pops open another window, then takes one of the ropes and tosses the rope to the first hostage. They move the rope to the top of the windows and tie off the rope. John takes the end of the rope and ties it around the ropes making them tight, and tosses the rope down the outside of the building.

Mac prone on the floor surveys the hallway, "One this is Three, ponder this. One, if you haven't made it back to the rally point, position between us to cover."

"This is One, I'm clear and moving to position."

The hostiles continued to advance down the hallway, each time one would break cover, Mac fired a few rounds to keep them pinned down.

Steve kept watch on the sides of the building while Don opened a notebook, picked up his satellite phone, "CHARLIE PAPA, CHARLIE PAPA, this is ALPHA TANGO, do you copy?" Don listened for a reply but only silence on the other end. "CHARLIE PAPA, CHARLIE PAPA, this is ALPHA TANGO, do you copy?"

* * * * * * * * * * * * * * *

Back in a dimly lit room sit two men, half asleep. The men all but fall out of their chairs.

One of the men grabs the mic and hollers, "Ted, get Mr. Smith now!" says Les, then pushes the button.

"ALPHA TANGO, ALPHA TANGO, this is CHARLIE PAPA, we copy, getting CHARLIE ACTUAL." Les releases the mic button and reaches for a recorder and turns it on as the speaker blares at him...

"CHARLIE PAPA, CHARLIE PAPA, be advised no time for ACTUAL, prepare to copy." says Don. The man grabs a note pad and a pen, and pushes the mic button.

"ALPHA TANGO, ALPHA TANGO, start SITREP." He releases the button and starts to write down the message.

"CHARLIE PAPA, SITREP as follows.... Contact made, hostages secured, two negative, three positive....be advised we Are Hot, We are

Hot….Need Extraction, Need Extraction ASAP! Do you copy?"

As the man writes out the message, the door opens and in walks a man and he hears the last message.

"ALPHA TANGO, ALPHA TANGO SITREP copied, standby for CHARLIE ACTUAL."

Mr. Smith walks over to the man and reads the message. He pulls the sheet of paper out of the pad and crumples it up in his hand.

"ALPHA TANGO, this is ACTUAL, unable to extract at this time, break contact, move to pre designated extraction, and await contact. Do you copy?"

"Message understood." Don reaches for his neck mic, "This is Two, copy following…be advised, we are on our own, need to get to extraction point ASAP."

****

Meanwhile, John has been busy getting the survivors hooked up and lowered to the ground. The first was the uninjured man. He was given the duty of protecting the survivors. He was to hold his ground until the others were lowered. The injured man was next, then the woman. As the third hostage was lowered to the ground, the gun fire down the hallway intensified. The guards were mounting an assault.

"John, we're about to have company," warns Mac.

"I'm ready."

Mac closed the door and used the AK to slide through the door handle and against the wall. Mac takes a corpse and uses his arm and chest as a wedge under the AK stock. He takes the remaining two claymores and places them between the wall and the body. Mac runs a dead man's wire to the dead guy so when he moves, the mines will detonate.

Mac moves to the window and hooks up the rope and carabiner. Mac slaps John's back, "GO, GO!"

John goes out the window head first and heads to the ground. Just as John has cleared the window the doorway explodes. Debris flies everywhere. Mac is thrown forward against the wall and bounces back to the right of the window.

The last thing Mac remembers before losing consciousness was lying on the floor, covered in debris. Ten men burst into the room, their weapons are searching for targets. One of the men moves directly to the window and is screaming as he points out the window. He motions for his men to give chase. The man grabs one of the men and gives him an order, "Get rid of the others!" and pushes him toward the door. The man stands at the window surveying the landscape.

****

As John starts his decent he can feel the blast behind him. He tries to look back but can only see the flash of an explosion. He hits the ground, unbuckles himself and looks toward the room he had just left. Nothing but smoke and flames.

John looks for Mac, but he is not there. John quickly gathered up the survivors and pointed them in the direction of their escape.

John points, "That way, run till you find our team. Go, go, go."

John takes the AK-47 from the man, just to be safe. Once they are moving, he follows providing rearguard.

"Two this is Four, do you copy?"

"Four this is Two we copy."

"We are on the move to you. Three is MIA!"

"We copy and are we are waiting, over." Replies Don. The group fades into the darkness.

* * * * * * * * * * * * * * *

Mac is dazed and lying on the ground, his ears are ringing but he can hear voices:

"GET UP Marine, we have dead and wounded. We have to secure the area." Mac looks up to see a Marine in dress blues; he is kneeling next to Mac.

The Marine yells again, "Are you just gonna lie there Marine and bat them baby blues eyes at me, or are you gonna get your ass in gear?"

"Yeah, Gunny, I'm good to go, thanks for asking."

When Mac gets up he realizes he is also wearing his dress blues. Mac looks around, realizes he's looking at the Marine Corps Barracks, he's back in Beirut. It's blown to crap: the dust, the smoke, the cries for

help. Everything goes dark again, his vision
blurs, the smoke clears. Mac can see people
standing by the window. There were two men
who resolved into one as his vision also
cleared. The man was leaning out of the
window screaming into a radio.

Mac slowly draws his Glock from its
holster, and then a silencer. Mac slowly and
carefully puts the silencer on the barrel.
Mac bumped it against a piece of debris. The
noise was slight, but it got the attention of
the man at the window. He turns toward Mac
and activates a flash light. He shines his
light searching for the source of the noise.
Mac extends the gun toward him. As the light
reaches Mac, the man can see him as Mac pulls
the trigger. The man's body makes a thump as
it hits the ground. Mac waits for a few
moments to see if anyone heard anything.

Mac clears the debris from around him,
finds his Stoner and heads toward the window.
Mac can't see anyone and can only hope John
was able to get them to the rally point. Mac
can hear screams and gunshots as he moves to
the door. Mac reaches for the mic of his
radio, "Two, this is Three, do you copy?"

Silence on the other end. Mac checks to make sure his weapon is hot, and then Mac checks the hallway. Clear. Mac moves toward the screams.

* * * * * * * * * * * * * * *

John and the hostages, moving in the darkness, are startled by the team. They take the wounded man and check his wounds.

John asks, "Any word from Mac?"

Dennis replies, "Nothing yet. We saw the fireworks, but haven't gotten any word from him." John shakes his head.

"We need to start making our way towards our extraction point." says Don, knowing that they are missing one and the effect it has on the team as a whole.

"I'm going to take rear guard and see if I can buy you and Mac sometime," John hands the man back his AK-47, "You may need this."

"Thanks, I'll do my best to help."

Don hands his M-4 with the M203 to John, "Just in case."

John takes it and gives Don his weapon, "Thanks, I'll return it soon."

The team gathers up their gear and head off into the darkness. John moves into the tree line for cover and gives the team some time to move out.

* * * * * * * * * * * * * * * *

The gunfire seemed to be coming from the floor below. Mac moved down the stairs to the third floor. The screams and gun shots are louder now. Mac moves to an open door. He sees a man stands in the middle of the room behind a line of people on their knees. Before the man can execute another person, Mac steps into the room, the man's back is to him. Mac can see three women kneeling facing the man. They see Mac and their startled look makes the man turn toward him.

"Drop your weapon" Mac tells the man. But he either doesn't understand Mac or just thinks he can win. He raises his weapon toward Mac. Mac unloads a burst into his chest, the man stumbles backward and onto the ground. Mac moves to the women and unties them. The women hug Mac and thank him for saving them.

• • •

"We aren't out of the woods yet. Stay here, let me check the hallway." Mac moves towards the door. As he reaches the door, in steps a man, wearing the uniform of a UN peacekeeper.

"I am an American here to rescue…" Mac never finishes his statement.

In one swift motion UN soldier raises a pistol and fires two rounds point blank at Mac. The first round hits Mac dead center in his chest, the second round lands just inches below the first. Mac's body shudders in pain as he falls backward on to the floor. Mac's weapon falls to the right of his body.

It takes a few moments for Mac's mind to clear, to regain his senses. Mac looks to his left and he can see the man standing in front of the three women who are again kneeling. The man is talking to them as he raises his handgun and points it at the first woman. Mac pulls his knife from its sheath, rotates toward the man then he swings it at the back of the man's legs, just above where his boot tops would be.

The blade slices through the calf muscles on both legs. The UN soldier screams in agony, the man's arm points toward the ceiling and he pulls the trigger multiple times. The man falls to the ground, writhing in pain. Mac rolls of on top of him, and grabs the hand with the gun. Mac drives his blade deep into the man's chest. Mac keeps the man's hand positioned toward the ceiling; it goes off again and again as the man's finger squeezes during his dying breath.

The women rush over to Mac to check on his wounds, but they can't find any, just some damage to his body armor. One of the women asks Mac, "How did you survived the gun shots?"

"I can only thank the maker of Dragon Skin." Mac takes his point and shoot camera out of his pouch and photographs the UN Soldier. Mac kneels next to the man and removes his name tag, UN patch and his UN ID card. Mac walks over to the first guard he encountered and photographs him also before removing his patches and ID. Mac also photographs the dead bodies that the man had executed before Mac killed him. Mac now knows why they were sent in and not the government.

With the women behind him, Mac checks the hallway. They move down the hallway to the stairway. Everything was clear so far. To the right is an open door to the outside. It just doesn't feel right, so they continue down one more level. Mac moves them through the door he had entered with John. Mac leads them to the window and Mac slowly climbs out. Once Mac was out on the ground the women follow.

"Stay low, be as quiet as you can, do what I say when I say it, and we just might survive."

* * * * * * * * * * * * * * *

John spots multiple targets, about twenty to twenty five, coming around the sides of the buildings. John loads the grenade launcher and lets the men get closer. The men are within fifty yards of his position when he pops off a round--Thump. The explosion lit up the sky about ten feet in front of a group of men. You could hear screams coming from the men. John reloads, lines up his next shot, Thump.

The explosion lit up the sky and swept away the guards moving away from the other side of the building. Mac hits the ground and the women do the same. Mac leaned up a bit trying to see what had happened, when he can see a number of men ahead of them moving away. They are firing into the darkness. Mac can hear the distinct sound of a Thump. He knows what is coming and tells the women to keep their heads down. Another explosion lights up the area. Again more screams and hollering. Mac scans the darkness in front of him looking for the position of the team.

As the fourth round is fired Mac can see the location from which it came. "One, this is three, do you copy?" Again, silence. The round landed in a group of about five and the explosion was deadly. Mac removes his flashlight and starts flashing a signal. Mac does this three or four times hoping they will see.

John is getting ready to fire again when he sees what he believes is a Morse Code message coming from in front of the building. John sends the round to the left of the signal, then one to the right of the signal. And the signal continues. John can't believe his eyes.

"One, this is Four, One this is Four do you copy?"

The radio crackles, "Four this is One, copy."

"One, you are not going to believe this, but I have a visual message from Three, and it reads, "This is Three, no radio, inbound plus three," and it keeps repeating."

"Four, I'm sending Five and Six back to help, we will keep moving, over."

"One, this is Four, copy."

Steve and Mark race back to meet up with John. John shows them were Mac is and they lay down cover fire around him. The hostiles have stopped advancing and are trying to engage the team. Mac tells the women, "Follow behind me about 10 steps. Stay low. If I go to the ground you need to go to the ground. If I don't get up wait till the firing stops and try and escape, the guards should be gone looking for the others."

The women indicate they understand and followed. Mac checks his weapon and moves slowly forward. As Mac reaches the guards they have their backs to him and don't realize he is there until Mac opens fire and kills one group at a time until he reaches the tree line. Once Mac reaches them they move to catch up with the others. It took them about forty minutes with the three women to catch up.

The extraction team of six has now grown to twelve: two additional men and four women. They rest for about half an hour. The team finds out the three women are doctors from the Doctors Without Borders. They were kidnapped from a local hospital on the border of Azerbaijan and Georgia. The doctors attend to the two wounded.

Mac broke the biggest surprise on the team. The guards in the building were UN soldiers, their involvement was why their team had been given this operation. Mac told them about the UN soldier who had shot him. He gave the patch and name tag to Dennis, "Here is the proof."

"Those bastards," Dennis looks to Steve, "That's why you're here isn't it?" Dennis moves to Steve and grabs him by the front of his BDU jacket. "What is your mission?" he yells. Don and John grab Dennis and Mark and Mac grab Steve and separate them.

Dennis grabs the satellite phone and a digital recorder. He plugs it into the phone and activates it. "Actual this is One, do you copy?" There is static and nothing. A few moments pass.

"One this is Actual." Dennis speaks into the satellite phone, "I'm only going to ask this once, CPS knew they were UN when you sent us in didn't you? And all the Intel, it wasn't just a coincidence that we got it so fast, and you planted your man in my team why?" The phone is silent…

"You are correct. They couldn't use US Military, so the government came to us for help. Our man is actually with the Agency. I don't know what his mission is. He is along for the ride. We have a bigger problem."

Dennis looked at the team. That look.

"Shit," Mark exclaims.

Actual continues, "The UN has reported a small group of terrorists has attacked a UN complex, killed an unconfirmed number of UN soldiers, and civilians. They are also reporting they have taken civilian hostages. They are going to hunt you with everything they have. The US Government has broken contact with us and is probably going to deny any participation in the rescue attempt if we can't prove it was corrupt faction of the UN."

Dennis struggles to speak without emotion, "The shit keeps getting deeper. Well, we have the proof. We just have to get it out. What options do we have?"

"Current options are limited. The UN is hunting you and our Government isn't saying anything."

Steve mouths, "We need to talk."

"Actual stand by." Dennis looks at Steve, "Okay, we're listening."

Steve gets a bit antsy. "What I am about to tell you is crucial to our National Security--let's just say I am not telling you this. This isn't how we had planned for this to go down, and you haven't even scratched the surface."

"Our original Intel was a rogue group of soldiers left over from the last Russian invasion. They were kidnapping and ransoming people, but after an exhaustive and costly covert investigation we found out they are old Russian underground, Eastern Orthodox Christians, old, old KGB!"

"They hate the UN, and they hate what Russia has become. They run as tribes for the Ola Anti-Marxist Soviets who fought with the US and French underground. These guys did the grunt work for the "Good" KGB, they were the hit men. They have actually been smuggling barrel-sized canisters of enriched uranium from Russia, through Georgia, to oil tankers in ports like Poti or Batumi. They hide the containers in the oil tanks and transport them to North Korea. They can travel unnoticed by our Navy. It wasn't until our telephone folks here were taken that we were able to track them here."

"They had been setting up listening posts at UN Bases which helped us gather this information. We are lucky because these rebels, still like to take hostages, but not for money anymore, they are rolling in it, but the women are for their personal pleasure."

Dennis returns to his conversation with Actual:

"We have a contingency plan. They think we will still head Southwest to Turkey where we were inserted. There will be activity to make them think that, but we will have to travel South to Armenia, cross into Iran, avoid the Iranian border patrols, travel West to Northern Iraq hook up with the Kurds and then to a Company airfield. We will then take a transport back to the states."

"Is that all?" says Don.

"It's the best I can offer," says Steve. Steve takes out his own satellite phone.

"Data retrieved, move to EP2."

"Confirmed, out." says a voice on the other end.

While Dennis was talking to Actual, Mac pulled Steve aside.

"Like it or not, you are a part of this team, no matter how you got on it. If you had pulled this shit in another time and place, you and your people would be dead, no ifs, ands or buts. This isn't another time or place, just remember that."

Steve's eyes were cold and unconcerned until Mac mentioned his people, his eyes glanced away as if looking for options or a response. Mac lets go of his arm, turned and walked away.

Dennis gets back to the satellite phone, "We have a contingency plan, better you don't know. Get us any satellite Intel you can on the UN's troop movements. Will contact you again in two hours, One out" Dennis put the phone away.

"Okay, we have a long and deadly road ahead. Don your on point, Mark and I will be front guard, Steve you're with the civilians, John and Mac, you have rear guard. Let's move out." states Dennis.

"Hey, who picked up my rucksack from the building?" Mac asks.

Steve reaches down next to him and picks up Mac's rucksack and tosses it to him.

"Thanks" says Mac as he grabs a full box of ammo and reloads the Stoner.

As the Team starts to move out Dennis takes Steve aside,

"You better be on the level and not pulling some spook scam."

"My neck is on the line, too," countered Steve.

CHAPTER 4

Realizations

It's 12:30 on Friday; Sandy is seated in a restaurant with some friends having lunch. They are having appetizers and talking about girl stuff. The restaurant has a bar area with TV's on different channels. The news is running on most of the channels, but Sandy doesn't really pay any attention to it as she continues talking. The local news turns to international news. One of the News Broadcasters catches Sandy's attention. Sandy looks up and watches the story unfolding on the TV:

"We have a breaking story from Tbilisi, the Capitol of Georgia. We now go live to their broadcast and a spokesman from the United Nations."

The screen flickers as it changes to a reporter, and a soldier dressed in camouflage and wearing a UN Blue Beret.

The soldier speaks to the reporter.

"We are currently searching for a group of men, men we have classified as terrorists. These terrorists have attacked a UN compound. These men are Americans, American soldiers!"

Sandy stops talking and walks toward the bar to hear the report. Her friends are still talking, but stop and watch her as she walks away.

"They have executed civilians, and killed UN soldiers attempting to protect those civilians. These terrorists have also taken a number of hostages. We will put all of our efforts into finding those hostages and returning them safely."

Sandy takes out her cell phone and dials a number and puts the phone to her ear. It rings a couple of times, and then she hears.

"The number you have dialed is currently unavailable, please try again later."

Sandy then dials Mac's work number, it rings once then she hears.

"The number you called has been disconnected or is no longer in service Please try again..."

Sandy closes the phone and turns back toward her friends, tears running down her cheeks. Her friends rush to her side and they all turn to watch the news report.

"The images you are about to see are disturbing."

The screen goes to images from around a building, showing bodies, both civilians and soldiers. The reporter turns away from the camera, "Commander, would you have time to."

He is interrupted by a second soldier. "Sir, you are needed immediately."

The Commander turns to the reporter, "I will give you more time later, right now I have an operation to conduct." He walks away with the other solider.

The reporter turns back to the camera.

"What I can tell you is that we have attempted to contact the US Military Command with NATO; they have denied any involvement in any terrorist attack. We hope to be able to bring you more as it becomes available." says the reporter. The screen goes back to the broadcaster.

"This is a horrible loss of life, we will be investigating and we will bring you more on this story as it becomes available."

* * * * * * * * * * * * * * *

As the UN Commander reaches their Hummer, they open the back doors and enter the vehicle. The driver starts the Hummer and they drive off. Inside the vehicle the two men are talking:

"I want these men found now! We cannot afford for them to be captured by anyone but us, you know the consequences if they are. Remember, there are others who are also watching to see what happens." Exclaims the Commander.

"We are doing everything we can. We have leads and are on the trail of these men," says the other soldier.

The Hummer stops next to a tent. The soldier opens the door and exits the vehicle, but before closing the door.

"We will find and kill them; we have all of our resources dedicated to it." The door closes, and the Hummer drives off. The soldier walks into the tent.

* * * * * * * * * * * * * * * *

The team is moving at a slow speed for them. They keep the pace of the slowest person while they are moving and scanning the areas around them. Mac and John are talking about inconsistencies in things they have seen and heard. They think they have a good idea of what is really going on.

The team has been on the move for about two hours when they stop again to give the civilians a break. Dr. Anna approaches Dennis.

"Alex and Cathy's injuries aren't life threatening, but more of a hindrance. Let me stay here with them, I can tend to them and you can move faster."

"Dr Anna, I appreciate your courage, but if I left you here you would all be dead as soon as they found you. I can speak for my team, and we would rather give our lives trying to save you than leave you here so we have a better chance of making it."

Dennis looks into Dr. Anna's eyes, "Mac once told me a quote from one of his favorite movies and it goes something like this; *All that is needed for Evil to triumph, is for good men do nothing.* Nothing is not an option." Tears run from the woman's eyes, she takes Dennis's hand in hers and kisses it. She then stands up and returns to the wounded.

The team is sitting around Dennis as he takes the satellite phone and tries to contact Actual again, but there is nothing. The phone acts like it is dead. As Dennis checks the battery, he sees there is no signal, no service. The phone has been turned off. Dennis looks to team and shakes his head.

"Nothing, they have shut us down, we are in the dark."

Steve takes his sat phone out and also tries to make contact, and again nothing. "Mines shut down too."

Mac looks around the team. "I have been going over this in my head and bouncing things off of John. Things don't add up, I have more questions than answers."

Steve pipes up. "We really don't have time to sit around the campfire and exchange stories, and we need to be moving."

John looks at Steve.

"That is pretty much what I expected you to say, this has to be said and will only take a few minutes."

"Let me tell everyone a scenario I have come up with and when I'm done you can fill in the blanks if there are any." says Mac.

"The CIA has all this Intel on private

company employees who just happen to get snatched by a group the CIA is actively monitoring. We, a private…oh hell we are hired guns, but more importantly not USA military or government agency, and are sent in to do the CIA's wet work. My proof, the telephone man was too adept in handling and using an AK. His comments weren't that of a telephone jockey. John found an incision on one of the dead bodies, and the first thing your man there did was to get to the bodies of his companions. You made a comment that data had been retrieved. Those so called telephone employees and you are really CIA operatives, and we were sent in to rescue or allow you to find some important evidence. How am I doing so far?"

The look on Steve's face says it all, "Damn they underestimated you Mac. Your investigative skills were wasted at the Police Department. The Secret Service should have taken you when they had the chance; age limit was the excuse they used when CPS asked them to pass on you."

Mac looking a bit surprised, maybe angry, that Steve knew so much about him.

Steve calls the three over. These are

Agents Mathews, Simpson and Young. They have gone to great lengths and sacrifices to collect and preserve this vital Intel."

Steve holds up two SD cards, they are a bit blood stained. Steve tosses both of the cards to Dennis.

"Everything I have told you is on each of those; it is your smoking gun. Documents, digital communications, photos, satellite images, and names of most everyone involved. You're the boss, I am your team member and they are at your service. But one last thing," Steve stands up. "Here is something for you to think about. We are and always have been on the same Team. It's like the Offense, Defense and Special teams of a football team; they work independently, but for the same goal." Mac angrily spouts, "This is the same kind of dishonest shit that made me leave the Corps and police work, now I have to deal with it here too! That's makes my decision easy." As Steve turns and walks away.

The discussion is over and Dennis approaches Mac, "I need your photo disk."

As Mac pulls out his camera and pops out

the card and hands it to Dennis with two fingers. Dennis starts to take it but Mac holds on.

"Do I get to know why?" asks Mac.

Dennis smiles, "Nope."

And he pulls the card out of Mac's fingers. He pats Mac on the arm. "Don't make a hasty decision until we know for sure." And Dennis walks away.

As the team prepares to move out, Dennis pulls Mark aside. "I need you to do something, something only you can do, something that could and probably will get you killed, something that if you succeed could save us. Something I can't order you to do, something that needs a volunteer."

Mark pats Dennis on the arm, "You know I will do anything you need, just say the word."

Dennis hands Mark two SD chips, a folded piece of paper and a GPS.

"You need to get this to our extraction point. Don't forget the trap we laid. The GPS location has been marked in it and will give off a low audible warning as you get close. Your best speed, eyes open and don't get shot or captured."

"Is that all", jests Mark.

"No, if you're not there on time at the EP, they may not come back a second time. Once you've made it back to the airfield email the information on that chip to the email address I have written down. Be sure to include everything I wrote down. All the information you need is there." says Dennis.

"I'll make it boss!" stated Mark.

Mark walks over to John and they talk for a minute. Mark strips off most of his gear, and then the brothers hug each other. Mark nods to Mac and fades into the darkness.

John goes through Mark's pack and takes the items he feels the Team might need and puts them in his own pack. He then tosses the pack into the trees. When it lands he walks over to it, pulls out a HE grenade, pulls the pin and sets it under the packs frame. He carefully moves away from the pack.

"Do you really think that is going to work?" asks Steve.

"Work? You bet your ass it will work, they are wannabies!" states John as he walks off to get his gear.

* * * * * * * * * * * * * * *

The Team has been on the move for some seven hours when Don returned from his advanced scouting.

"There is a clearing about one hundred yards ahead, and you're going to want to see this." says Don.

Don leads Dennis and Steve through the dark woods until they come to the clearing. All three men look beyond the clearing to see a roadway. Although it is still dark they can see hundreds of headlights.

"I don't think we are going to be able to get through that with our injured and civilians." says Don.

"Can't we ever catch a break!" murmured Dennis. The men return to the others. "Well there is a large clearing ahead and," Dennis hesitates, "There is no easy way to say this there are hundreds of troop transports, jeeps and tanks. It's a staging point for their search to find us."

* * * * * * * * * * * * * * *

Mark has been on the move now for about

eight hours. He stops for a moment to catch his breath. His progress has been inconsistent. He stops often to check his surroundings and to make sure he hasn't been followed or isn't running into an ambush. Mark knows he has less than a day to make it to the extraction point. Mark is up and moving again, searching the darkness for any signs of danger.

* * * * * * * * * * * * * * *

Tim and Jack are conducting the preflight check at the Huey when three men dressed in fatigues walk up to them.

"You have not been cleared for flight ops, you are to stand down until advised otherwise." says one of the men.

Tim and Jack both stop what they are doing and walk toward the men. "We are scheduled for a pick up run in a couple of hours." says Jack.

"We have not received any confirmation that they are there, headed there or even alive. You will stand down until you are given clearance." the man states firmly.

"Who the hell do you think you are?

Those are our men out there, we are scheduled to get them, and I don't care if they are there or not. We will go out every night till they are and there isn't a damn thing you can do to stop us!" states Tim.

The man hands Tim a satellite phone. Tim takes it and puts it to his ear. "Yeah." says Tim. The voice on the other end is Smith, he is short and clear, "You will stand down until I say otherwise, are we clear?"

"Crystal" Tim tosses the phone back to the uniformed thug. The three men turn and walk away.

"Son of a bitch!" shouts Tim.

Jack looks puzzled as he asks Tim what happened.

"That was Smith, he ordered us to stand down until he says otherwise."

"Something is not right." says Jack as he turns and walks back to his barracks.

Tim sits down in the open door of the Huey and shakes his head.

* * * * * * * * * * * * * * *

Mac winces as Dennis is telling the others what was ahead.

"Sometimes I'm so stupid." Mac says.

John chuckles, "What is it?"

They move away from the group. Mac drops his back pack and pulls out a satellite phone.

"Yeah, okay it doesn't work remember?" says John.

"No that was their sat phones…this one is mine." Mac smiles. What Mac just said got John's attention.

Mac turns on the sat phone, and dials. It rings, but no one answers, then, a beep.

"MacDaddy this is AT3, sitrep is hot! Pick up for one at EP as scheduled, must have SatLap." Mac leaves a voice message.

Mac looks to John. "Don't say anything to the others yet, I don't want to get their hopes up, but I left a sat phone for Tim under the seat in the Huey. I know it's against regs, but I do it every mission. I hope the beeping will help him find it."

* * * * * * * * * * * * * * *

Tim is sitting in the open door of the Huey. Jack walks out into the hanger and hollers. "Come on, it's chow time, we can work on a plan while we eat." Tim gets up and walks toward Jack. Jack and Tim head inside the hanger building.

There is a ringing coming from the Huey.

CHAPTER 5

Misdirection

Once through the chow line, Tim and Jack head to an empty table away from the others where they can talk. They sit there eating and looking around at the soldiers and other personnel in the chow hall assessing everyone's probable affiliation. Some are some active duty Air Force personnel who obviously run and maintain the air field, some pilot types around, they are military, but unsure if they are US Military, as well as groups which aren't current US military but are on someone's payroll.

"We have to find a way to get to the extraction point." says Tim.

Jack shakes his head in agreement, "With or without authorization!"

The men pick up their glasses and tip them to each other.

"I'm not sure what other options are available to get us there, but I will take a look around and see." says Jack. The men continue to eat their meal.

****

Once Dennis is finished talking, Steve breaks out a map.

"With this group in front of us, I don't think we can make it any further south. If it were just your Team, I'm pretty sure you could make it. But not with my banged up group and the doctors. It is too dangerous, and we have come a long way to not make it."

"What do you suggest?" asks Don.

"If I may," say Dennis, "it is obvious; somehow, they think we are headed south. We know they are in front of us and they have troops behind us, it is just a matter of time before we get sandwiched. We need to head East back toward Turkey, back to our original extraction point. If anyone doesn't agree, speak now, or we move."

Everyone looks around at each other, but no one speaks.

"Let's move." says Don.

As Dennis starts to move into the woods, Mac grabs his arm.

"We all know this is going to go bad fast. You guys need time, plain and simple.

I'm going to stay here and use what I can to make them think we are still here, keep them busy to give you time to get to the EP."
Dennis starts to say something.

"I'm not asking Dennis!" states Mac.

"I'm staying also." says John.

"As much as I wish you could, you can't. You have to make sure they get out. I will catch up." Mac tells John.

The group goes through their gear gathering up any grenades, explosives and trip wires they still have. Mac shakes hands with the team members; the Doctors thank him with their eyes. They know what he is about to do.

As Mac he is sorting out the supplies, figuring out what is there and how he can use it. He ridicules himself, "Sure, Mac, play the hero. Save the day by sacrificing yourself….Idiot!"

There isn't much there to use, so Mac moves closer to the trucks parked less than fifty yards from him. As he crawls toward the trucks between the trees and bushes he scans for hostiles and anything he can use to ruin someone's day.

* * * * * * * * * * * * * * *

Daybreak illuminates a group of about twelve to fifteen armed men. Moving slowly they scan the woods for any signs of the men they are hunting. One of the UN soldiers stops and moves toward an object in the tree line. As he picks up the backpack one of the men behind him and slightly to his left realizes what the man is doing and yells "NO!"

The yell dissolves into an explosion which shatters the quiet of early morning.

The other men scatter as the explosion sends debris flying in all directions. The man who had picked up the pack is torn into pieces as he takes the brunt of the explosion. As the smoke and dirt settle, the men scramble to see who is dead or injured, they find three of their group with moderate injuries, and one man was missing more of himself than was there. They setup a perimeter and tend to their wounded.

* * * * * * * * * * * * * * * *

As the sun was starting to rise and the darkness was slowly turning to daylight. Mac set the last of his booby traps. Mac seated himself just inside the brush line about fifty yards from the vehicles, and a temporary camp the UN soldiers had put up. Mac was about to attach the trip wire to the pin on the HE grenade he had tied to the base of a bush, when he sensed someone approaching. Mac got as small as he could and as close as he could to the bushes. Mac's back was against the brush. Mac could see two men approaching, and could barely hear them. One of the men motioned to the other and he started to walk away from him and toward Mac.

Mac reached down to draw his knife, but it wasn't there. He looked toward a tree where he had left his stuff while he was setting up the traps. There was his Stoner and his knife where he left it after pre-cutting the grenade tie downs.

The UN soldier is standing next to Mac. The UN soldier leans his AK on a tree and unzips his pants. He relieves himself on the bush Mac is hiding under. Mac slowly reaches into his left cargo pants pocket and pulls out a wire object. The UN soldier sighs as he finishes. Once he zips his pants back up he get out a pack of cigarettes. He slaps the pack on his hand and pulls one out. He places it in his mouth and starts looking for his lighter.

Mac slowly rolls to his left and is on his hands and knees. Mac gets into a crouched position and places the ends of his wire object in each hand. As the soldier lights his cigarette Mac jumps up and in one motion crosses his forearms and puts the wire over the head of the man in front of him. Mac pulls his arms back to his body, causing the wire to tighten around the neck of the man. The man is startled; he tries to cry out but is unable. The soldier tried to use his fingers to get between the wire and his neck, but is unable. He reaches for his weapon and Mac jumps backward pulling the man to the ground with him. As Mac and the man are falling backward Mac wraps his legs around the arms and body of the man. Mac pulls harder until the soldier is no longer struggling, then he pulls harder to make sure he is dead. Mac rolls the man off of him and grabs the AK. He scans for the other man, but doesn't see him. Mac lays the weapon down next to him, rolls up his garrote and places it back in his pocket. He then attaches the last trip wire to the grenade pin. Once attached, he straightens the cotter pin. Mac grabs the AK and grabs the collar of the dead man and drags him back toward the tree where he left his equipment. Once at the tree Mac gathers his gear up. He knows it's a matter of time before the trailing group shows up or the friends of this man come looking for him. Mac looks in the direction of the camp, then in the direction of the soldiers following him. He then looks at the dead guy and smiles, "Good idea, even if I do say so myself."

Mac moves the man up against the tree in a sitting position and takes the parachute cord and lashes him to the tree. He places the AK in the dead man's hands and using the trip wire lashes it to his hand and to the knee. Mac bends the dead man's knee up and ties the knees to the tree so it won't bend.

Mac runs to the other side of his traps and attaches a new wire around a tree and back toward the dead soldier. Mac grabs a branch and bends it toward him and attaches the wire to the tree. He then runs the wire inside the trigger housing and around the handle and makes a slip knot. He attaches this end to the branch. Mac pats the dead soldier's shoulder, "Happy hunting." Mac grabs his gear and disappears into the woods making sure his path is easy to follow and avoiding any of the surprises he has just setup.

****

The sun is starting to rise and you can see a man standing behind a tree holding an AK 47. He is watching a man jogging towards him. The man stops and is looking at a device in his hand. Mark is looking at the GPS. He looks around trying to get his bearings. A man with an AK 47 steps out from behind a tree with his AK pointed at Marks head. The Man speaks and startles Mark. Mark puts the GPS in his shirt pocket turns toward the man with his hands raised.

"Drop your weapon and turn around," says the man in Russian, but Mark doesn't understand.

The man gestures, speaks, "Move, move." Mark gets the idea that he is supposed to move in that direction. Mark moves slowly and the man becomes agitated. He puts the barrel of the gun in the middle of Marks back and pushes.

Mark feeling the pressure where the barrel was turns to his left quickly, his left arm still raised, and his right arm falls to his side and draws his side arm. The left arm knocks the barrel of the AK but doesn't move it off its target. The man struggles to keep the barrel pointed at the man and squeezes the trigger, the AK fires, Mark feels a slight burning in his right shoulder. His right hand drives the Glock side arm into the chest of the man and Mark squeezes the trigger three times. The rounds rip through the man and his limp body falls to the ground.

Mark can hear people yelling behind him. He looks and sees movement. Mark picks up the man's AK and starts firing in the direction of the people. The AK's bolt stops firing, Mark tosses the AK to the ground and pulls two grenades from the man's web gear. He pulls the pins and tosses them. Mark grabs his M4 and starts running as the grenades explode behind him, he has gained a little breathing space.

The others, a group of ten men approach the area and find their fallen comrade. The commander shouts out his orders. The others take off into the woods after Mark.

Mark is in pain, his shoulder is throbbing and bleeding. Mark has his M4 in one hand and the GPS in the other as he runs through the woods. The screen on the GPS shows his position a blinking red dot. The two are close and getting closer. The GPS is beeping as Mark stops and looks around for the markers they left to show the mines. Mark is exhausted, he struggles to locate them. He moves carefully to them one at a time and turns them around. Once they are turned he has to relocate the trip wire. Mark focuses all his attention on safely executing the task.

The men following Mark are moving fast. They know they aren't far behind him. Their numbers make them careless focused on the chase.

Mark knows he is only about four hours from the extraction point and has no time to rest. As Mark gets on his feet he sees the men rushing toward him. Mark raises his M4 and lets loose a full magazine into the oncoming men. Three of the ten men fall, the seven remaining keep coming and start firing at Mark. Mark turns and starts to run as he reloads his M4. Mark can hear the bullets passing by him and the near misses hitting the trees and leaves. Mark turns slightly and points his M4 behind him and let's loose controlled bursts.

Mark takes about three steps before he hears an explosion and feels a sharp pain as he tumbles to the ground.

Mark can hear the other explosions annihilating the remaining seven men; their bodies had been torn to pieces by the four mines. Mark, wounded and bleeding, struggles to sit up. He searches is pack for his med kit. He finds his quick clot and applies it to his shoulder wound and his leg wound. Mark wraps it as best he can before he gets to his feet. He knows he knows he may not have a lot of time, to deal with two possible deadlines. Once on his feet he fades into the woods again.

****

Jack and Tim finish their meals. Jack
tells Tim he is going to head back and check
on their chopper.

"While you are doing that, I'm going to
look around at the other aircraft in the
facility that might be of use to them." says
Tim. As both men get up, he pats Tim on the
arm, "I'll catch up with you later." as they
both walk in different directions. Tim
investigated different hangers, but only
groups of fighters and large cargo planes. He
was about to call it a night when he hears
the props of what sounds to be a helicopter,
but are much louder and more powerful. There
sits an Osprey, its rotor blades turning,
winding down. Tim opens the door and walks
in. Once the blades stop, two men walk out of
the open rear hatch. Tim walks toward them.

"Damn, I have heard about this, but I
have never seen one." The two men look at
each other and start to walk toward Tim.

"This is a restricted area, I'm sorry
but you will have to leave."

Tim holds up his hand, "Okay just a
second." He reaches into a pocket and pulls

out a couple of items, he shuffles through them till he finds the one he wants. He puts the rest back in his pocket presenting an ID card to the two men.

"Not to worry gents, I am authorized." The two men look at the ID card and badge and then at each other. "No problem sir, look around, if we can answer any questions just let us know." The three men walk around the plane and talk about the attributes of the Osprey.

CHAPTER 6

Missed Call

Jack inspects the Huey's exterior, then climbs in and sits on the interior floor plate as he visually inspects the interior structure. As he starts to climb out he hears a beep. Jack climbs back in looking for the source of the beep. Then there is another beep. Jack looks under the seats and finds a bag. Inside it he finds a Satellite phone and its charger. The phone's battery is low, and it shows one message. Jack pushes the button to get the message. As Jack listens to the message his eyes widen, he jumps out of the Huey. "Gotta get Tim."

* * * * * * * * * * * * * * * *

Mark reaches the extraction point, wounded, losing blood and exhausted. Mark finds a tree that faces the clearing and sits against it. He pulls out a smoke grenade and sets it down next to him. He places his M4 in his lap and checks to make sure it has a new mag. He clicks on the mic, "ET, ET, this is AT Five do you copy?" Silence

"ET, ET, this is AT Five do you copy?"

* * * * * * * * * * * * * * *

Jack finds Tim walking away from a hanger, and shouts "We have to move now!"

"What's up?" asks Tim.

Jack hands Tim the Satellite phone, "I found this under your seat, and you need to hear the message."

Tim recognizes the voice, *"MacDaddy this is AT Three, sitrep is hot! Pick up for one at EP as scheduled, must have SatLap."* Tim and Jack look at their watches and then each other.

"That was four hours ago." Says Tim.

"I'll get the laptop, you get the Huey ready." says Jack running to the barracks. Tim tries to dial the only number in the phone recent missed call list but no answer. Tim heads to the Huey to prep for flight.

Tim has the rotors on the Huey spinning as Jack arrives with a bag. Jack gets in and straps up. As the blades increase in speed, Tim spies a group of men approaching them; these are the same men who made them stand down the day before. Tim fast tracks his warm up and the Huey springs off into the air. Tim and Jack can hear the Control Tower recalling them, but ignore them, changing the radio frequency to AT's coms.

Jack tries the coms, "AT, AT this is ET, do you copy?" They know they have a three hour flight to the EP. They hope they are in time.

****

The UN soldiers are moving slowly through the woods, their numbers are now at ten. One died from the explosion, three were injured and one man stayed to tend to them and await medical treatment. The men come to a break in the woods, it's not a clearing, but the trees and bushes are thinned out.

As they scan the area they see what they think is a man sleeping leaned up against a tree. They open fire on the man and move toward him. Their adrenalin has taken over, they have forgotten their last engagement. They rush in. The first trip wire releases a branch that springs back, squeezing the trigger. Causing the weapon to fire. The branch reaches it furthest point of momentum and swings back, releasing the grip on the trigger. The gun stops firing.

* * * * * * * * * * * * * * *

The majority of the UN camp is at chow in the mess hall, when they are surprised by the gun fire so close. The UN soldiers scramble to gather their weapons and head toward the gunfire. As they move through the clearing they trigger the trip wires placed on that side. Two explosions rip through the body of five men. They fall to the ground. The rest of the camp's soldiers push forward, firing their weapons indiscriminately. Another group of men trip the wires killing three soldiers. They move for cover and open up on the other end of the clearing.

The tree branch returns to its normal position and again pulls the trigger back, firing the AK until it runs out of ammunition. The booby trapped man takes round after round. Both groups keep pressing their attack. The soldiers from the UN camp are the last ones standing. The gun fire from the pursuing group has stopped.

• • •

The UN soldiers check the area and find the soldier tied to the tree, and the other soldiers....UN soldiers. The body count is staggering. The camp lost twenty men and the other group lost all ten. The Commander stands in the middle of the kill zone hollering in Russian. Soldiers are scrambling around tending to the wounded.

One soldier reports to the Commander. "We have found a trail where a number of people have gone off into the woods."

"Hand pick two squads and follow it. Watch the ground for trip wires, find these men and KILL them." The Commander walks back toward the camp. The one soldier hollers out names and two squads of men gather around him. He hollers out orders to them and then they follow him into the woods.

****

Tim and Jack have been flying for almost three hours. Jack is still trying to raise the Team on the radio. "AT, AT, this is ET, we are ETA five, do you copy?"

Then instead of static they get a faint response. "ET, ET, this is AT Five, hostiles unknown, popping smoke."

Mark uses the last of his strength to pull the pin on the grenade and toss it into the clearing.

"AT Five we have blue smoke, inbound ETA five mikes." says Tim. "Jack, man the M60 just in case. Once we land I'll get Five while you cover us."

"Roger" says Jack as he climbs out of the pilot seat and into the crew area. Jack racks a round into the M-60 and starts scanning for hostiles.

The Huey approaches the smoke; Tim is looking for AT Five. He spots a man sitting and leaning against a tree. Tim puts the Huey down as close as he can. The rotors are still spinning as Tim jumps out of the chopper and runs toward the man. As Tim reaches Mark, he shouts his name. Mark doesn't move. Tim grabs him by the vest and pulls him up over his shoulder, grabs his M4 and heads back to the Huey. Tim lays Mark on the floor of the chopper and gets back inside the pilots chair. Jack leaves the M60, and is trying to tend to Marks wounds. Tim spins up the rotors and they are airborne and headed back to the air field.

Mark is barely conscious. He starts to say something but doesn't finish his statement. "He's alive, but has lost a lot of blood, I've got to stabilize him." Jack works intently to stop the bleeding. He rides all the way back holding Mark, talking to him, telling him to not give up and to hang on.

****

The two squads of men slowly head into the woods. The point man is scanning the ground for trip wires or traps. The men behind him are watching him intently for any signs of danger. Their weapon are in various positions, some holding them at their waist, some pointed up resting on their shoulders, as they scan the woods around them.

One of the soldiers whose AK-47 is pointed up resting on his shoulder is walking when he feels a tug on his weapon. Thinking it's just a branch he pulls his weapon and all he hears is "tink". A soldiers knows the sound as the pin of a grenade is pulled and the safety lever is released allowing striking pin to light the fuse. The soldier knows he only has seconds to live. He pushes forward against the other soldiers, "GRENADE" as the explosion tears through the bodies of the men. After the dust and debris settles the survivors tend to the wounded.

* * * * * * * * * * * * * * *

As the Huey approaches the airfield, Tim turns the radio back to its frequency.

"Flight control this is JoyRide we are inbound with one, we need medical on the tarmac. Do you copy?"

"JoyRide this is Flight control your flight was not…"

Tim cuts off the transmission, "I don't give a rat's ass if we had authorization or not we are inbound and we need medical on arrival." states Tim. "We are clear JoyRide, medical will be waiting, over." says Fight control.

The Huey comes in over the trees and sets down. The medical Team approaches the Huey and they tend to Mark. They off load him and rush him to the base medical facility.

Tim and Jack are approached by five uniformed soldiers.

"I am Major Nichols and you are being placed on restrictions for your unauthorized flight."

Tim gets in the face of the Major, "I don't give a shit who you are. I don't work for you and you have NO authority over us. I'm going to check on our Team member" as he and Jack walk past the group of soldiers. One of the soldiers starts to move toward Tim and Jack, but is stopped by the Major. "Watch them. Don't let them out of your sight." The Major walks off and the four soldiers follow Tim and Jack.

****

Don is on point and John has fallen back to cover the teams rear. Dennis, Steve, Agents Mathews, Young and Simpson are protecting the three Doctors as they stop to tend the wounded. Don slowly moves back through the woods to the Team. Don motions to Dennis.

"It doesn't look good. The woods break and there is a large clearing about three hundred yards wide and twice as long. We can go around, stay in cover but." says Don

"I know, they are exhausted and are barely moving now. Any slower and we will be moving backwards." says Dennis.

Don looks at the ground. "Im going to regret telling you this, but there is an old stone and concrete building close to the far side of the clearing. It's not in real good shape, but might give us shelter to rest. It looks like there is a well too. We can see anyone approaching, but it puts us in a very bad tactical position. We won't have any cover to escape if it came to it."

Don wipes the sweat off of his face with his hand.

Dennis clicks his radio, "This is One, I need Four and Six here now."

Steve is the first to reach Dennis and it takes John about ten minutes.

"Okay, here is the situation. Steve I need you to leave one of your men with John here in the woods as eyes. At dusk we will move to the house Don found. Steve I will need another one of your agents to move to the other side of the clearing for eyes. The rest of us will keep watch, and rest up. We will move out of the house before first light and continue on to our extraction."

"Will do Boss," say John as he moves out back into the woods.

Steve starts to say something but stops at the glare he got from Don. Steve moves to tell Simpson to go with John and inform Mathews of his assignment. The Team waits for darkness to move.

As night falls the team moves slowly into the clearing. The group reaches the building.

Steve takes off his mic and gives it to Mathew.

"Listen, keep your eyes open, let us know what you see." Mathews gives Steve a sarcastic smile.

"Keep your head down." says Steve.

"I will." Mathews, continues to the tree line to set up eyes. The doctors find a corner and are asleep before they lay their heads down. Don gathers Dennis, Steve and Young together.

"Okay, we will work in two man shifts, two sleep, two on watch. Dennis you and Steve sleep first. Young and I will stand watch.

We will do two hour intervals and see how that goes. Dennis and Steve crash out to get sleep. Young gathers up the camelbacks and canteens and moves to the well. She drops the bucket down the well and pulls up a bucket of nice cold water and fills the containers.

CHAPTER 7

Re-enforcements

Standing inside the woods is a man dressed in camo. He is scanning the field with binoculars. The silhouette of a person catches his attention. He concentrates on the area in which he saw a shadow. The man picks up a radio, "Control, Control, this is check point Down's Farm, do you copy?" There is static.

"Down's Farm we copy, over."

"Advise we have movement in the field, again we have movement, over."

"Copy Down's Farm, keep watch." The coms officer puts down the radio, and heads out of the communications tent.

* * * * * * * * * * * * * * *

"Down's Farm, Down's Farm…" shouts the man as he is running towards another man who is standing at the door to another tent. He runs up to the man. He is out of breath but trying to pass along a message. Once he catches his breath, "Captain, we found them!" The Captain instructs the man to find Sr.

Sgt. Vladimir, have him report to the Generals tent immediately. The Captain enters the Command tent.

"Vlad, Vlad…" shouts the man as he stands at the door to a tent and beating on the post. Vladimir finishes getting his pants on, opens the door, "What is so.."

"My apologies Sergeant but you are to proceed to the General's tent, Now!" says the soldier. Sgt. Vladimir starts running in that direction, struggling to put his jacket on.

As Sr. Sgt. Valdimir reaches the door to the tent he knocks on the post and waits for an answer. Captain Andre Mihailov walks up to the tent.

"Reporting as ordered, Sir?" asks Vlad.

"Enter" shouts a man from inside the tent. Vlad opens the door as Captain Mihailov enters the tent first, there is a man putting on his uniform shirt and walking to a desk.

"Sir, my apologies, but I knew you would want to hear this immediately."

"Yes, yes what is it Andre?" grunts the man.

"I believe we have found them, we have a report at Down's Farm." The mention of this gets the General's attention.

"Send a platoon, send five platoons of your best to Down's Farm. Kill them all, leave no one alive. Do you understand?"

"Yes Sir!"

"Andre, if you fail, I will kill you myself." the General threatens. The two men leave the tent.

"Gather the men Senior Sergeant we move NOW!" says Andre.

Vlad runs off and starts shouting commands. Men rush to five trucks with their weapons and gear. The trucks are on the move within a half hour of the command to form up.

* * * * * * * * * * * * * * *

Tim and Jack are in Marks recovery room. Two soldiers stand watch outside the door.

It's been almost six hours now since Mark came out of surgery; Tim and Jack are still in his room, waiting for Mark to wake up. Jack is asleep in a chair, snoring loudly. Tim stands at a window looking outside. Mark's eyes open, "Damn, you make it hard to get some needed sleep with that racket!"

Tim turns around to see a smile on Mark's face. Tim whacks Jack on the head to wake him up.

"What, what…I wasn't snoring!" exclaims Jack.

"Oh, look sleeping beauty is awake."

"How is everybody? When can I see them?" asks Mark.

Jack and Tim look at each other then back to Mark.

"Um we are doing fine and this is it." states Tim in a puzzled voice.

"NO!" exclaims Mark, "My brother, the team, the others?"

"Mark, you're it! We haven't heard from anyone else." says Jack.

Mark tries to sit up in bed. "I gave you the disk and their location; you were supposed to upload the information and pick them up!" says Mark with urgency in his voice. Tim helps Mark to sit up.

"Once we got you in the chopper, you passed out. You have been out for about nine hours." explains Tim.

"No, that can't be, they are counting on me to get them out." Mark is in a panic.

"We have to leave now, where is my uniform, the GPS?" asks Mark. Jack hands Mark a bag with his uniform and gear in it. Mark starts searching for something.

Mark searches through his uniform in the bag and pulls out a folded piece of paper. Mark unfolds it to reveal two disks. He hands the blood stained disks and the note to Jack. "You must upload this now, it has to be sent now; their lives depend on it." Jack grabs the laptop case, turns on the computer, and places the SD cards in the PC and opens up the files. Jack is amazed at the information he is looking at.

"Tim, you're not gonna believe what is on here!" Jack initiates the email program and types in the addresses.

The lists of address are to the CPS, CIA, NSA, FOX News and the UN.

Mark hands Jack the second disk, "This and the information on the first disk go to those emails and this unnamed address." He puts the information in the note into the message.

"Oh man this is gonna get dicey!" says Jack as he sends the information. He hands the laptop to Tim who reads it and looks at both Jack and Mark.

Jack moves toward the door, "I'll see if we can get the Huey fueled and authorization for an op."

Mark stops Jack, "The Huey won't be big enough for everyone." Both Jack and Tim say,

"It was big enough to get the Team in."

"Oh I guess I didn't tell you that either did I?"

"Nope." says Jack and Tim in unison.

"Better fill us in." says Tim.

Mark explains about the three doctors and the three phone employees who are actually CIA operators they rescued, that the Team went from six to twelve and there are still eleven to be picked up. Jack and Tim look at each other and smile. Together they say, "The Osprey!"

* * * * * * * * * * * * * * * *

It is early morning when the trucks arrive. The trucks stop a mile or so from the farm and the men jump out. Vlad gathers the men. "Bust your asses to get to the observation point. If you were in truck one you have the left flank. Truck two, you have the right flank. Truck three you have the middle. The other two trucks will wait until I call for you. Once you are in position we will start our attack, and the trucks will come for support." The men take off down the road toward the observation point.

* * * * * * * * * * * * * * *

Jack and Tim stand up from their chairs. "Give us about a half hour before you send the email and make the call. We should have lost our escort and be ready to take off." Tim tells Mark. Mark nods and they all shake hands. As Jack and Tim walk out the door they see their escort sitting down the hall.

Jack waves to the escort, "What time do they start serving chow?" The Escort stands up and starts walking toward them.

The escort looks at his watch," its zero four hundred, in about an hour."

"Great we have time, we need to stop and get someone." says Tim. The two men followed by the escort out into the compound.

* * * * * * * * * * * * * * *

John is sleeping and Simpson is supposed to be on watch, but has fallen asleep. John snaps awake, he looks around to see Simpson asleep. But his attention is drawn to the wooded darkness in front of him. He can't hear anything, it's more a sense. John reaches over and puts his hand over Simpson's mouth, then shakes him. Simpson makes a noise, but it is muffled by John's hand.

"One and Two, this is Four do you copy?" There was silence on the mic. "One and Two, this is Four, DANGER close, I repeat DANGER close!" The mic is still silent for a moment.

"Four copy, do you have visual?" asks Don.

"Negative, it's just a feeling, I'm moving to investigate, over."

"Affirmative. Advise ASAP." Don jolted Dennis and Steve out of their sleep and advised them. They wake the others.

The light of dawn begins to push back the darkness. Dennis, Don and Steve are surveying the tree line in front and around them trying to get a visual on John's "feeling." It doesn't take long for that "feeling" to become a reality. Moving just inside the tree line, they can make out movement that can only be bad for them. Dennis clicks on the mic button, His voice is soft, but loud enough for everyone in his Team to hear.

"CONTACT, multiple contacts in the tree line, prepare to defend this position. Conserve your ammo, this is going to get ugly fast."

* * * * * * * * * * * * * * *

Vlad, directs his men into position, and gives the order to attack. His men have taken cover in the trees and open fire on the concrete and stone building. The sounds are deafening as the AK's fire on full auto. These men aren't worried about ammo.

* * * * * * * * * * * * * * *

The bullets fly over head, striking the front of the building, shearing off parts of the stone. It sounds like rain on a tin roof pounding down on them. Dennis, Don and Steve try to return fire. But they know it is only a matter of time before they are overrun.

Simpson has moved to the edge of the tree line across from the buildings trying not to be seen. John is advancing trying to get position on the hostiles.

* * * * * * * * * * * * * * * *

Vlad picks up the radio, "Send me my trucks."

The man on the other end of the radio, signals to the other two trucks. They head out down the road to the observation point.

* * * * * * * * * * * * * * * *

Tim heads to the building to speak with Tony the Osprey pilot. One escort had stayed at the hospital door while the other guy followed Tim and Jack. Now the escort had to make a choice and followed Tim when the two men split up. Tim knocked on the door to Tony's apartment. It is dark, but then a light turns on and the door opens. Tony is startled when Tim just walks in puts his hand over Tony's mouth and closes the door behind him.

Tim whispers "I'm sorry to do this, but I need your help. I don't have time to explain, our teams lives depend on your help."

Tony nods his head in acknowledgement.

"What is it you need from me?" asks Tony.

"Get your flight gear, and is there a back door out of here?" Tony puts on his pants, grabbed his gear and leads Tim to the back door.

Tim is trying to explain to Tony what is going on as them make their way to the hanger.

Jack walks to the hanger where the Osprey is kept and picks the lock on the door. He goes in and turns on the lights. He moves to the rear of the Osprey and makes sure there is plenty of ammo for the ramp-mounted machine gun. Jack looks up as the door opens and Tim and Tony enter. Tony heads to the cockpit and begins the pre-flight inspection.

Everything is ready. Jack hits the button to open the hanger door and runs up the ramp as it begins to close. Tony is in the pilot's seat, Tim is the co-pilot. They have both put on their night vision. The Osprey begins to move out of the hanger. Tony reaches up and flips a toggle switch to deactivate the external lights. He turns his head toward Tim and speaks into the mic. "No one needs to see us." and he smiles.

　　The Osprey is now clear of the hanger. The blades are spinning at full power and rotating into the vertical lift off position. The Osprey jumps off the tarmac and roars into the darkness. Tim is impressed by the power of the plane. Tony tells them to hang on as he drops the blades into flight position. The transition is flawless; the Osprey goes from a helicopter to a rotary plane moving just above the tree tops.

* * * * * * * * * * * * * * * *

　　In the flight ops command center there is a beeping as a plane is detected on the radar. One of the men in the room picks up a phone and dials. He waits for someone to answer. "Sir we have an unidentified aircraft that has left without authorization." He

pauses, "no, it's not a helicopter, yes sir."
And he hangs up the phone.

★★★★★★★★★★★★★★★★

Mac runs through the woods, and then
there is a road in front of him. Mac scans
for any signs of friends or foe. Mac slowly
breaks cover moves onto the dirt road with
signs of recent vehicle movement. Mac moves
to the other side into the woods and
continues to follow the road. Mac can now
hear faint automatic gunfire off in the
distance. Mac comes to a stop and takes cover
as he hears trucks. Mac looks to his left and
sees two trucks moving toward him on the
road. The trucks reach him and continue past
him down the road in the direction of the gun
fire. Mac picks up the pace and tries to
reach the team on the radio, but only gets
static.

★★★★★★★★★★★★★★★★

Vlad bellows out commands, directing two
of the platoons to break off and flank the
enemy's position. Two platoons start to move

• • •

out in opposite directions. The third platoon maintains their small arms fire on the team's position.

* * * * * * * * * * * * * * *

The Osprey is flying low to avoid radar. Tim is looking at the GPS and a map where Mark indicated the Team was heading. They weren't far away, so Tim changes the radio's frequency and tries to make contact. "Alpha Tango, Alpha Tango, this is JoyRide do you copy?" There is static on the radio. Tim keeps trying to contact the Team.

* * * * * * * * * * * * * * *

Debris flies everywhere as the rounds strike the building. Dennis, Don, Steve and Young are randomly firing through windows, cracks in the walls and doorways. The Doctors are huddled in the corner; thinking the end is near. All they can hear is the sounds of bullets flying over, the buzzing, the hissing, the thwacks, the thuds from impacts to the building and the impacting of surfaces around them. The crack, crack, crack sounds from the teams weapons as they fire back and the pinging sounds from the brass shell casings as they bounce on the ground.

The radio crackles, everyone is straining to hear who or what is being said. "...this is three, ... two trucks loaded .....headed in ....Do you copy."

John replies, "Three this is Four, partial copy, you are breaking up, over."

John looks at Dennis who shrug's. John presses his mic, "Information broken, two trucks loaded headed, and that's all I could get."

Dennis passes the information onto Don and Steve. Dennis activates his mic, "Sounds like we have more company coming, this party is about to get crowded."

****

As the trucks arrive Vlad is shouting out orders to the men to fall in with the main force at the farmhouse. The men rush to the line and join their comrades. The newly formed assault force moves out of the woods into the clearing. Their guns are blazing on the structure; they only see occasional muzzle flashes coming from the enemy. The rounds are not aimed and most of them never find their mark.

* * * * * * * * * * * * * * * *

Mac stops on the top of a small hill, surveying the ground in front of him: five trucks, two of which are partially out of the woods in the clearing, two men manning what looks to be an M-60 machine guns atop those two trucks, sixty men advancing out of the trees into the clearing. He sees one man on a radio giving what looks to be directions, he must be the commander. Mac looks in the direction the man is pointing and sees men moving through the woods to flank the clearing. He knows he is close to his team. Mac moves to try and help the others.

* * * * * * * * * * * * * * * *

John has reached a position about one hundred yards from where he left Simpson. John sees approximately thirty soldiers headed to his location through the woods.

John heads back towards Simpson's location but on a little wider arc.

"One and Two, this is Four, do you copy" says John.

"Four, this is Two, go."

"Confirmed! Twenty to thirty hostiles attempting to flank your position headed right toward us, over."

"Copy last, Four. Move to defensive position. You are on your own, we have our own problems, over" states Don.

"Copy Two, we are on our own!" John turns and moves at a fast pace to get to Simpson so they can find a good defensive location.

Steve taps Dennis on the shoulder and points toward Mathew's last location, "You can bet they are coming on both sides."

"Um, this is Mathews, I copied that and moving."

"Clear," says Dennis to Steve, "Mathews is aware and on the move."

****

"Alpha Tango, Alpha Tango, this is JoyRide we are inbound, do you copy?"

"JoyRide, we copy, we are HOT! I repeat, we are HOT! What is your ETA?" asks Don.

"ETA is thirty to forty-five minutes, copy?" says Tim.

"JoyRide, we copy, thirty to forty-five..." the mic is still keyed up, and there is silence for a few moments as he looks at the doctors sitting in the corner, "We don't have." There is silence on the radio. "Guys, thirty, will be too long, we are about to be overrun, copy."

"We will make it, I promise." says Tim as he looks to Tony, "Can we get there?" Tony shakes his head, "Maybe, barely, but it will put us on radar."

"Do what you have to." The Osprey engines roar as it climbs in altitude. The lower to the ground the slower the plane flies, but it doesn't show up on radar. The higher up, it can move faster, but it can be seen on radar.

****

Back at the UN command post a uniformed soldier runs out of one of the tents. He runs to another tent and bursts in the door. A man sitting behind a desk stops his work and looks up to the man.

"My apologies General, but this is urgent, for your eyes only." The man holds out a piece of paper. The man behind the desk motions for him to bring it to him. He takes the paper and reads it. He stands up and yells for Andre. A man enters the room.

"We have a problem, an aircraft is inbound towards Down's Farm, it must be a rescue attempt." states the General.

"I will have two attack helicopters dispatched to intercept it and stop any rescue." states Andre.

"They better not fail Andre!" Andre turns and he gets on a phone as he exits the building.

CHAPTER 8

One way trip

Back in Turkey, at the Company's airfield, the command tower has been monitoring the Osprey on radar. One of the flight control agents pick up a phone and it is answered on the other end.

"Are you sure?" asks the man. The flight control agent,

"Yes sir they have scrambled two aircraft, I believe them to be attack choppers, from a UN field and are headed in an intercept course for our guys."

"Clear, I'll get back to you." says the man as he hangs up the phone. The man picks up a satellite phone and dials a number. The phone is answered on the other end.

"I need an off the books combat mission, no questions asked!"

Moments later, blasting over the intercom is a siren, "This is not a drill, I say again, this is not a drill! This is a Dark Angel authorized mission, Raptor 218, Raptor 343 on mission." The base comes alive, men scrambling to get to their designated posts.

As the two pilots gear up they are met by Major Nichols. He hands them both sealed envelopes. "These are your orders and target, good hunting." He turns and walks away.

The men finish getting ready and head for their fighters. As the fighter pilots reach their planes, they climb into the cockpits, with the canopies still open they power up.

Once they start to taxi to the runway they close the canopies. The planes sit side by side as they wait for their clearance. The speakers in their head sets come alive. "Your designation is now Dark Angel 218 and 343, you are authorized weapons hot, over."

"Dark Angel 218 Clear."

"Dark Angel 343, clear." Is their reply into the coms.

"Good hunting." The two pilots look at each other, give the thumbs up. The Raptors engines come alive as they head down the runway and into the sky.

****

"JoyRide, JoyRide this is Flight Control, do you copy?" Tony and Tim look at each other surprised to hear flight control on this channel. Tony activated his coms.

"Flight Control this is JoyRide, we copy?"

"Be advised we are tracking two, I repeat, two inbound hostiles, your location. Believe they are attack choppers to spoil your pickup, copy."

"We copy, don't have anything on scope yet," says Tony.

"Be advised you have an inbound Dark Angel mission to cover your six, copy."

"We copy Flight Control"

"Bring our boys home." Tony, Tim and now Jack are looking at each other as the coms go quiet.

"I guess Mark got their attention," says Jack.

* * * * * * * * * * * * * * *

Mac reached the trucks undetected. It was easy since everyone's attention is directed in front of him. As Mac approaches the man that looks to be in command and two other soldiers, he puts the shoulder harness of his Stoner over his head and lets it hang on his back next to his pack.

Mac draws his Glock and puts on a silencer. Vlad and two men stand their looking at the battlefield, congratulating themselves on what seems to be a victory for them. One of Vlads Lieutenants notices Mac, and turns toward him as he raises his AK. Mac is already prepared. He points and fires his weapon with calm precision. The round strikes the man in the forehead and he falls limp to the ground. The other two men turn and realize what is happening. Vlad pushes the Lieutenant toward Mac, as a human shield, as he starts to run away. Mac takes aim and puts two in the chest of the second man. Mac's attention is then turned to Vlad who has run out into the clearing toward his advancing soldiers.

Mac looks to the trucks and the two machine guns firing down at the building in the clearing. Mac moves to the closest truck, he climbs up on the bed and approaches the man firing the weapon. Mac looks to his left at the other man operating the machine gun. That man sees Mac, their eyes meet. Mac can see the man trying to decide on what to do.

As the man starts to turn the M-60 toward him, Mac fires his weapon and the man falls into the bed of the truck. Mac turns to the man in front of him; he fires one round into the base of the skull. The man slumps over the machine gun. Mac grabs the man by his collar and pulls him off the gun.

Mac holsters his pistol and mans the M60. Mac looks for Vlad who has now reached his men and he is trying to get them to turn and fire back toward the trucks. Mac pulls the trigger. Tut, tut, tut....hot lead flies toward the soldiers. Vlad takes the brunt of the volley, his body spins and falls to the ground. The soldiers closest to Vlad also take rounds and are killed. Mac keeps firing on the soldiers in front of him. The soldiers realize where the rounds are coming from and are turning to return fire in the direction of the trucks. Rounds are ricocheting off the front of the truck and flying over Mac. Mac's attention is focused in front of him and he doesn't notice the soldiers flanking him from the right until the rounds start landing around him. The wood from the railings on the truck is exploding in splinters. Mac takes a round in the right side of his vest and it knocks him to his knees. He realizes he is in trouble and scrambles to get up. He grabs the dead gunner's body off the bed of the truck and lifts him up and leans him over the railing as a barrier.

* * * * * * * * * * * * * * * *

Dennis and the others began firing at the soldiers, catching them in a crude crossfire as they scramble to decide who is the greater threat. The advancing soldier's numbers split between both targets.

"Alpha Tango, Alpha Tango this is JoyRide do you copy?" There is no answer just static. "Alpha Tango, Alpha Tango this is JoyRide do you copy?" This time there is an answer.

"JoyRide, JoyRide we copy, over!"

"We need smoke for location, do you copy?" says Tony. Don puts down his weapon and is digging through a rucksack. He pulls out a smoke grenade. Don looks to the trees to see what direction the wind is blowing. There is a slight breeze from behind them. Don Pulls the pin, releases the safety lever and tosses the grenade out in front of their position. "Bang" goes the grenade as it spews out red smoke. The smoke rises into the air marking their location.

Dennis picks up the radio, "Popped red, do you have visual?"

Tim points to a distant clearing ahead of them, "Affirmativ,e we have red smoke, about two miles out. Over."

"We copy, JoyRide, be advised we are very hot."

"JoyRide is clear, coming in hot!" says Tim. Tim clicks on his fight coms, "Jack, I'm opening the hatch." Tim flips a switch on the console and the rear hatch starts to open. The light from the outside illuminates Jack standing at the open hatch of the Osprey manning an M240D. Jack locks and loads the weapon, "Weapon hot!" he says into the coms.

The Osprey blazes in over the clearing and begins its transformation from a plane to a rotor blade. As the Osprey approaches, it maneuvers the bay toward the hostiles on the ground. Jack opens fire. They now have even more lead raining down on them. But they are also giving it back. The Osprey is taking rounds.

****

Mac is back up and firing the M60, alternating from the front to his right trying to keep the soldiers preoccupied as the rest of the Team prepares for their escape. Mac is surprised to see the Osprey as it disappears behind the smoke, but even more surprised as he scans back to his right and sees a soldier out in the open with what looks to be a GP-30, 40mm grenade launcher, mounted under the AK barrel. His fear is realized as he sees the flash and smoke pop from the weapon. Mac abandons the machine gun and turns to jump out of the truck to avoid the explosion. The round is short, but lands under the truck. The initial explosion wouldn't have been so bad but it ignites and explodes the fuel tank of the vehicle.

The truck lifts off the ground in a fiery ball and rotates toward the other truck. Mac is just starting to jump and thrown forward from the explosion over the second truck and lands hard on the ground on his left side. Mac lays there stunned and suffering from the concussion of the blast and probably broken ribs from the fall.

John sees the explosion and knows Mac is in trouble. He knows he is the only one that can help him. He looks to Agent Simpson to tell him to cover him, but he sees him breaking from cover and running out into the open toward the landing aircraft. John yells for him to stop but Simpson keeps running. John shakes his head and starts to turn his attention back to Mac when he sees Simpson go down. Simpson is on the ground and flailing around in pain, the bullets still landing around him. John, not knowing Mac's condition, knows he has to help the injured agent and takes off in the direction of Simpson.

Dennis is giving directions. He tells Don and Young to make sure the Doctors are the first to get on the Osprey, that they need to guard them with their lives. Don and Young acknowledge their assignments. Dennis tells them, "He and Steve will provide cover fire for their escape."

Tony lands the aircraft behind the team's location, putting the bay toward the Team to make their entry as easy as possible. Jack lets go of the M240D and picks up an M4 and steps out of the bay. He uses the weapon

to fire at targets of opportunity as he waits
for the team.

★★★★★★★★★★★★★★★

Two men stand over Mac's body, they poke
him with the barrels of their AK's. One of
the men is intrigued by the weapon hanging on
Mac's shoulder. He reaches down and turns Mac
over to get the strap off. Mac rolls on his
back, his right arm flops over but stops in
mid arc. Mac's eyes open and their eyes lock.
The man's eyes open wide as he realizes it's
not a dead body. The man looks to the other
soldier their eyes meet as the other soldier
looks down and also realizes they are in
trouble. Mac pulls the trigger and two rounds
rip into the chest of the man standing over
him. The man violently jerks as his body
falls backward. The other soldier is
scrambling to get his weapon up to use, he
looks down at Mac and sees the flash from the
barrel of the gun and his body falls to the
ground. Mac struggles to his hands and knees
and tries to get up but can't. Mac starts to
crawl toward any cover he can find.

* * * * * * * * * * * * * * * * *

Jack can see five people coming toward him. One of them goes down, clutching their leg. It is Agent Young on the ground with a leg wound. Doctor Anna is the first to her aid. Don tells them to get on the plane; he will take care of Young. Don picks up Young and puts her over his shoulder and heads to the plane. Jack directs them into the cargo bay as he continues to fire at the enemy.

Dennis signals to Mathews to make a break for the plane. Mathews doesn't hesitate and beats feet to the cargo bay, firing off his hip as he runs.

Dennis and Steve are still trying to provide cover fire as they see John helping Agent Simpson toward the plan. Once John and Simpson have reached the plane Dennis and Steve start their run to the plane. The smoke has all but dissipated. It worked both as a locator for their rescue and for the two approaching attack helicopters. The helicopters have located the rescue plane and start their attack run.

Dark Angel 218 and 343 are screaming across the sky. They know it is going to be close as the radar shows the bogies have reached JoyRide. The pilots are just within lock-on range of their weapons and each pilot takes a target. As doors opens on the side of the Raptors, missiles rotate into firing position. Out flies an AIM-120C and it's off down range toward its target. Both pilots advise Fox-3 away over the radio. The Raptors continue to make sure they hit their marks.

The first attack chopper takes aim and fires two rockets toward the team. The rockets are off their mark and explode between the Osprey and the stone structure. As the second chopper lines up to fire the first helicopter explodes. The pilot looks in front of him and the last thing he sees is the missile as it strikes the canopy and explodes. The debris from both helicopters fall to the ground in flames.

"Flight Ops, splash two, Dark Angels out" says Dark Angel 218, and both plans do barrel rolls and head back to base.

The smoke clears from the violet explosions. Dennis and Steve lay on the ground, neither is moving. Jack screams, "Men down." John and Jack head to their team members. Jack reaches Dennis first, he is breathing but there is blood everywhere. Jack grabs Dennis by the collar and takes off running dragging Dennis behind him. John reaches Steve only seconds later. Steve isn't breathing and he knows he has to get him to the plane. John grabs Steve and lifts him up and over his shoulder and heads to the cargo bay.

Mac can hear everything on the radio, as he is dragging himself to cover and safety. Mac knows he is alone and they can't help him.

"JoyRide this is Three do you copy?" It takes a moment, but JoyRide answers.

"Three this is JoyRide, hang on we will have you out ASAP." says Tim.

"Negative JoyRide, I say again negative, nothing you can do for me right now, you have wounded that need immediate medical."

Tim cuts in on the radio, "No chance Three, we are coming for you."

Mac shakes his head and spits out blood. "Two this is Three do you copy?"

Don answers, "Go Three."

"You and I both know the reality here...I'm hurt, hurt bad, I know it's a one way ride, you have to do what is best for the team." says Mac, as he is coughing and spitting up blood.

Don looks at Tim then keys his mic, "JoyRide, take off, Three stay alive. We'll be back." Tim tries to argue with Don, but Tony takes off. The rounds strike the Osprey as it transitions back into a plane and heads away from Mac.

Mac keys his mic, "Tim, you promised," then static.

"You stay alive, I don't care how, but you stay alive. I will be back!" says Tim. "John, find Shane, he's on deployment!" says Mac and the radio goes silent.

CHAPTER 9

SecNav

In the cargo bay doctor Karen is addressing the others wounds, while Doctor's Anna and Michelle are working fast to save Dennis and Steve's lives. They have a medical kit, but nothing for the injuries they are facing. Doctor Anna tells Don, "We need a trauma center if they have any chance of surviving. We can stabilize them for a short time, but it is imperative that it is soon!"

Tim changes the frequency on the radio, "Flight Ops, this is JoyRide do you copy, over?"

Moments later, "JoyRide this is Flight Ops we copy." says Major Nichols.

"Advise if you have a level one trauma center?" asks Tim.

"Negative JoyRide, we do not. I can give you two options, one of which is a UN base and isn't advisable under your current status. As for the other, I'm not telling you this but it is at the following coordinates and frequency."

Tim writes down the information. "Flight Ops, we are clear and thank you, JoyRide out."

Tony puts in the coordinates then looks at Tim. "Um, that's in the Med."

Let's try to raise them and advise them we are inbound, don't want to surprise them and get shot down! Let's see who answers" says Tony.

"Mayday, Mayday, Mayday, this is rescue flight designate JoyRide in bound your location, do you copy?" There is nothing but static. Tim repeats, "Mayday, Mayday, Mayday, this is rescue flight designate JoyRide in bound your location, do you copy?"

"THIS IS AN UNAUTHORIED TRANSMISSION ON A SECURE CHANNEL, CEASE TRANSMISSIONS!" Tim and Tony look at each other and shake their heads.

"Now what" asks Tony.

"Hang on, I'll be right back." Tim gets up from his seat and moves to the cargo bay. He kneels next to Don, "Here is the situation; we got nowhere to land with the medical facilities we need. The one option we had is telling up to piss off. Right now we need one of Dennis's contacts to save our asses, do you know any?" asks Tim.

Don looks at Tim and shakes his head, "The ones I know can't help us out here." Tim's head slumps down:

"I don't know what to do, we left Mac, and we have men dying."

Young is sitting in one of the seats as Doctor Karen is bandaging her leg but has to stop as she moves closer to Tim and Don, "I might be able to help." Tim and Don's interest is peaked and they look to her. "My uncle might be able to help us if I can get hold of him."

"Your uncle?" asks Don in a funny way. "My uncle is the SecNav! You know, the Secretary of the Navy, and YES, he really is my uncle." says Young with a smile. Tim and Don look at each other and smile.

"Her uncle is the SecNav!" they both say in unison. Tim hands her a satellite phone.

"Save our asses Agent Young!" says Tim. Agent Young dials a number into the phone and waits as the phone connects.

* * * * * * * * * * * * * * * *

The soldiers regrouped, gathered up the dead and tend to the wounded. A group of the soldiers are searching around the trucks looking for the American's body but it's not there. They begin searching the area but find nothing. Then one of the soldiers finds a track or trail leading into the brush. As they follow it they come across Mac who is passed out from his wounds. The soldiers pick him up, remove his gear and weapons and drag him back toward the trucks. Once back at the trucks the soldiers load up their wounded in one truck and in the other, they place their dead and tie each of Mac's wrists to the cover rails. The remaining soldiers load up and head back to their base.

* * * * * * * * * * * * * * * *

The radar operator is scans the monitor, he leans back, "Skipper, our contact has not changed course and is still on an intercept with us. Their range is two hundred miles." The Skipper walks over to the radar operator.

"Where are our fighters?" he asks.

"Currently on a refuel op on the opposite end of the scope from the unidentified contact." says the radar operator.

"Scramble the Alert Fighters!" says the Captain.

Somewhere in the Mediterranean Sea, general quarters sounds on a carrier. The carrier comes to life as the crew scramble to their battle stations. Two fighters are sitting on the flight deck ready to launch. The two F-18 Super Hornets are catapulted down the flight deck, once airborne the two fighter's engines come to life as they disappear into the horizon.

The Skipper is on the radio giving combat instructions to the alert aircraft, "Alert Five, this is USS Ronald Reagan Actual, do you copy?" There is static on the radio.

"Ronald Reagan this is Alert Five, read you five by five, over." The Skipper continues his conversation as the radio operator receives an incoming emergency communication on a secure line. All the radio operator can say is, "Yes Sir, Yes Sir, one moment Sir, while I get him." The radio operator covers the speaker on the hand unit. "Skipper this message is for you."

The Skipper turns to the radio operator, "Can't you see I'm a bit tied up right now." barks the Captain at the radio operator. "But sir, this" is all he can get out before the Captain interrupts him, "Give it to the XO."

The radio operator looking scared to death speaks into the hand held unit, "One moment, sir," and hands the receiver to the XO.

"This is the XO.." is all he can get out. The XO snaps to attention and his head jerks toward the captain. Their eyes meet and the Captain knows there is a problem as he moves toward the XO. The XO hands the receiver to the Captain, "It's the SecNav!"

The Skipper takes the receiver and as he raises it to his ear, he glares at the radio operator. "This is" and he stops talking. "Yes sir, Yes Sir, Yes Sir, full and complete assistance, Yes Sir, anything they need, Yes Sir."

The Skipper hands the receiver to the radio operator; he looks to the XO and starts to say something, but stops. The Captain returns to the radio operator, raise JoyRide, and advise them to continue their path. They will be escorted by our fighters.

Tim and Tony look at each other and start laughing..."I guess we are authorized now!" they say in unison. With the carrier in view they lower the landing gear. The F-18's fly cover as the Osprey transitions from flight to vertical landing. Once on the deck there is a Medical Team waiting to take the injured. As Don and John exit the aircraft they are met by the Captain. "I'm looking for whoever is in charge." Don steps up and starts to salute then stops himself, "Sorry, old habits." He then extends his hand, the Captain does the same, "Well he is lying on that gurney headed to surgery." says Don.

"I have been instructed to provide you with any and all assistance you may require." states the Captain.

While Don and the Captain are talking, John steps up and extends his hand to the Captain and they shake hands. Don introduces John, "Captain, this is John, and yes we need your help. Is there somewhere we can go to talk?" The Captain motions toward the Bridge, "This way gentlemen, we can use the ready room."

Once on the bridge, the Captain asks the Executive Officer, (XO), and the Command Master Chief, (CMC), to join them in the Captain's ready room. The XO closes the door.

"We have a man still on the field. His last transmission was that he is injured and sacrificed his rescue for our safety. The last request he made was for us to find Shane, if it is the Shane I think Mac was referring to, he is Master Chief Shane Myers with one of the SEAL Teams that are currently deployed." says Don.

The Captain instructs the XO to locate the Master Chief. The CMC speaks up, "If I may Skipper, I believe Team Five is already on board." Everyone looks to the CMC. The CMC snaps to. "I will get him, Skipper." The Captain smiles as the CMC exits the ready room.

The CMC traversed the corridors of the carrier to reach the squad room were the SEAL Team is assigned. As the CMC enters the room the SEALs start to snap to attention, then they realize it is just the CMC. "Stand easy SEALs, it's just our illustrious CMC." says Master Chief Myers.

The CMC makes a face about his announcement, as he looks around the room. The two officers, a Lieutenant and a Captain, approach the CMC from behind him. The CMC's eyes meet with the Master Chief's, "The Skipper wants to see you." The Captain says, "Roger, is he on the Bridge, CMC?"

The CMC turns and looks confused at the Captain. "Not you, Captain Spear. He wants the Master Chief. But, you better come along, I have a feeling you will be asked to join us." The CMC exits the squad room followed by Master Chief Myers and Captain Spear.

* * * * * * * * * * * * * * * *

Inside the tent, Major General Tarasov is seated behind his desk with two other men dressed in regular clothing. One of the men speaks up, "When you informed me you had one of the Americans, I thought he was here. How much longer must we wait till they arrive with him?"

"Comrade Uri, I notified you as soon as I was informed. It shouldn't be too much longer." Just as he finishes speaking, a truck comes to a stop outside the tent. Its dark out, the lights from the trucks illuminate the area as men jump down from the truck and they untie their prisoner and drag him into the tent. Once inside the tent, they drop him on the floor. Mac lies there motionless.

Tarasov stands up from his chair and walks to the front of his desk. He grabs a chair and drags it near the man lying on the floor. He motions to two of the men to put him in the chair. One uniformed soldier and one man dressed in regular clothing take an arm and lift him up, the man in regular clothing has Mac's right arm, and the UN soldier takes the left arm. They lift him up and drag him toward the chair. Mac's hands are free; they think he is unconscious. His right hand slides up to the shoulder holster of the man in regular clothing. Mac's left hand finds the UN soldier's side arm located on his right hip. As the two men drop Mac onto the chair, he unsnaps the holsters of both men and draws the pistols as they release his arms. Mac's arms fall down to his side. As the two men are standing in front of Mac getting ready to walk away they notice Mac's head raise slightly, they can see Mac's eye looking up at them. The two men panic, they reach for their weapons but they are not there. Mac is holding a gun in each hand in front of his chest. He smiles at the two men, extends his arm toward the two men and fires. The two men fall backward. The other two men are surprised by what just happened. Mac stands up pointing a gun at the remaining two men. "So which one of you has the most influence and can get me out." asks Mac. The two men start talking over each other trying to make a case for themselves. "Screw it" says Mac, he pulls both triggers and both men fall to the ground. Mac hears some commotion outside the tent. He takes the utility knife off the UN soldier and moves to the far wall. He takes the knife and cuts his way through the tent as a group of men enter the tent door. Mac fades into the darkness.

* * * * * * * * * * * * * * * *

The CMC reaches the ready room, opens the door and motions the Master Chief to enter. "Stand by Captain, I'm sure you will be joining us shortly." says the CMC. He enters the room and closes the hatch. "This is Master Chief Shane Myers, I believe he is the one you are looking for." says the CMC.

Master Chief Myers sees Don and knows he has met him before. "Skipper, permission to ask why I am here?" says the Master Chief.

"Stand Easy Master Chief, these are friends and at the direction of SecNav they have asked to speak to you." stated the Captain.

"Aye Aye Sir." says Myers.

Don extends his hand to the Master Chief. "You probably don't remember me. I only have a slight recollection of you. Mac introduced us a few years ago when we were in Coronado."

The master Chief shakes his head as if to acknowledge he remembers. "Mac is down in hostile ground; his last transmission was to find you. Can you tell us why?" asks Don.

The Master Chief looks at everyone and shakes his head. "No Sir, I don't know right this moment. But I will figure it out."

The Captain turns to the XO, "Get the SEAL Team Captain up here." The XO goes for the secure line.

"If I may Skipper, Captain Spear is outside the hatch, I figured you would need him at some point." states the CMC. "Damn you really are the goat on the boat. Bring him in." says the Skipper with a smile. The CMC opens the hatch and summons the SEAL Team Captain.

"Okay, gentlemen, here is the long and the short of it. SecNav has given specific directions that our guests here get whatever they need, no questions asked. If they ask it, it is as if the SecNav has asked it, are we clear!" states the Skipper, "Now I'm going to leave you to sort out what it is you need and how it is you will get it done. XO, you are me for this meeting. Keep me up to date." says the Skipper as he and the CMC exit the ready room.

John speaks up, "We have to get Mac back. Like you, we never leave a man behind."

"Okay here is what we know...." says Don as he begins to explain the operation from the beginning to the two SEALs without leaving out a detail.

* * * * * * * * * * * * * * *

UN soldiers are moving about trying to figure out what was going on. Mac moves from shadow to shadow, making slices in the tents as he goes, then back tracks and continues in a different direction to cover his trail as he tries to make his escape. He comes to the end of one tent and is about to move to the next tent which is about ten feet from him, when Mac sees 2 UN soldiers approaching him. Mac steps out of the shadows and startles the 2 UN soldiers. They are slow to react. Mac has the knife in his right hand at his waist. In one swift motion Mac thrusts it in an upward motion into the neck just under the jaw of the man in front of him to his right and draws a pistol from his waist band with his left hand. The knife severs the spinal cord as the man falls lifeless to the ground without a sound. He points the gun at the man's face. The UN soldier freezes. Mac puts his index finger in front of his mouth, "Live or die, the choice is yours." The UN soldier raises his hands,

"Live."

Mac orders the soldier to remove his BDU jacket. As the UN soldier finishes removing the jacket, Mac takes his right hand and strikes the UN soldier on the chin! The soldier falls to the ground. Mac puts on the

BDU jacket and picks up his UN beret, puts it on and moves back out into the shadows.

CHAPTER 10

Feet Dry

Twilight was fast fading, the deck of the USS Ronald Reagan was just becoming illuminated, the elevator from the flight deck was rising. On the elevator deck was sixteen SEALs and John, geared for action. Once the deck was in place they move toward the Osprey that is sitting on the flight deck. Tim and Tony stand outside the Osprey. The SEAL Team heads to the ramp and board the Osprey. John and the Master Chief approach Tim and Tony, "Guys this is Master Chief Shane Myers. Master Chief this is our flight crew." Tim and Tony shake Shane's hand, "You are going to find Mac right?" asks Tim.

"We are going to do everything we can Sir." states Shane. The Master Chief and John walk up the ramp and take a seat inside the Osprey. Tim and Tony enter the cockpit and fire up the rotors. The Osprey lifts off and heads to Mac's last know location.

****

Don is in the corridor outside of the sick bay, leaning against a bulkhead when one of the ships doctors approaches him. Don stands tall and extends his hand to the doctor. The two men shake hands. Don looks concerned as the doctor's face shows sorrow or sadness. "What's the word Commander?" asks Don. The Commander looks Don in the eyes, "The two with minor wounds will be fine, but for the others it's not good news, Sir. My apologies, but I only have first names for the patients. Steve succumbed to his injuries on the table. We were able to save Dennis, but there are concerns about his injuries." says the Commander.

Don's head lowers, and he looks to the floor. "How bad is it?" asks Don.

"The shrapnel we pulled out of his lower back did major damage to the muscles and came very close to his spinal cord. We have repaired everything we can, he still has some shrapnel in him, but now it is up to him and time." advised the Commander.

"Can I see him?" asks Don.

"Soon Sir, right now he is in recovery and needs his rest." states the Commander.

Don looks at the Commander, "Altman, Steve's last name was Altman, Staff Sergeant, U.S. Army Rangers, Retired, and it's Dennis Jennings, at this time that's all I can tell you."

The Commander thanks Don for the information and walks away. Don leans back on the bulkhead and gets out his satellite phone and dials a number.

* * * * * * * * * * * * * * * *

In the cargo hold of the Osprey, Captain Spear sets out his plan for the initial search, "I will lead Team One, we will secure the LZ and provide security. Although Lt. Block will be a part of Team Two, Team Two will be led by MC Myers. His Team will conduct the search efforts. John, you and Chief Carison will be with Team Two, Chief Reid you're with me."

The Osprey flies just above the tree tops as it enters a large clearing. Tim points to the building the Team had been held up at, then to the tree line a hundred yards or so in front of it, "Put her down as close to that spot as possible." says Tim to Tony. The ramp opens up and the SEAL Team stands ready to exit the aircraft. Once the Osprey lands the SEALs and John exit the ramp. Captain Spear is the first off the aircraft and he directs his Team to setup a perimeter. The other Team heads into the tree line. "Petty Officer Thomas," barks Capt. Spear. The Petty Officer Runs up to the Captain who is still standing on the ramp. "Get a message to the Ronald Reagan, Feet Dry." "Aye, Aye." says Petty Officer Thomas as he heads into the Osprey.

The team moves slowly into the tree line. They scan the area for any signs of Mac. Lt. Block clicks his throat mic, "Found something." Lt. Block signals for the team to follow, he has located a truck that had been blown up and was sitting on its side. As the Team reaches the truck they spread out looking for anything that might tell them what happened to Mac. John and MC Myers are near Lt. Block. "This is the truck Mac was firing a M-60 from." says John.

As the group is scouring the area, Chief Carison is busy looking for tracks or indications in the ground. He moves slowly away from the group. Moments later Chief Carrison broke the silence on the mic, "I found his gear." Everyone stops and look around to see where he is. "Head north forty yards into the heavy brush, you will find me." states Chief Carison.

The team moves in the direction they were given. It took them a few minutes to reach Chief Carison who was kneeling next to some gear. Chief Carison stands up holding a flack vest and a Stoner. "Damn they left all his gear." says one of the SEALs. "There is a lot of dried blood here, I'd estimate it to be eight to twelve hours old." states Chief Carison as he turns and looks for MC Myers. He locates him moving through the bush and moves toward him. MC Myers stops and turns back toward the team, "They drug him to here and loaded him into a truck and headed east."

They gather up the rest of Mac's gear and head toward the Osprey. John starts to gather up Mac's gear from the guys. He approaches Chief Carison, "Can I get Mac's stuff, Chief?" says John. Chief Carison walks past John holding Mac's vest, pack and Stoner. John looks kinda puzzled at Chief

Carison and starts to say something when MC Myers puts his hand on John's arm. John turns toward the Master Chief. "Mac's stuff will be fine, for right now let him hang on to it." says MC Myers. John starts to say something to MC Myers. "It's important that he has some time."

John interrupts MC Myers, "Um, what's the deal, Chief, he needs some time?"

MC Myers puts his hand on John's shoulder, "Chief Carison is Mac's son!" states MC Myers as he continues to walk to the Osprey. John turns toward the team and stands there dumbfounded.

The team loads back into the Osprey and it lifts off the ground and transitions into flight. The flight seamed to last for hours as John sat there looking at Chief Carison. John wanted to talk to him about his dad, but didn't know how to start the conversation. By the time he had an idea what he was going to say the Osprey transitioned to a vertical landing and the cargo bay doors opened. As the Osprey came to rest Capt. Spear stands, "This is a show of force, Teams One and Two on the deck with your weapons ready. You are to stand guard until MC Myers, Chief Carison, and I return. If confronted, DO NOT stand down! Consider this a hot LZ!" The SEAL's exit down the ramp. They setup a perimeter around the Osprey, weapons at the ready. Capt. Spear turns and walks down the ramp followed by Chief Carison and MC Myers. Capt. Spear stops at the bottom of the ramp, "Lt. Block, Petty Officer Thomas!" The Lt. approaches Capt. Block as Petty Officer Thomas runs up.

"Yes sir."

I want you and Petty Officer Thomas to go to their communications tent, make contact with the Reagan, let them know what we have found." Captain Spear reaches into the cargo pocket of his pants and pulls out an item. He tosses it to Petty Officer Thomas, "Plant this so we know what they know."

Petty Officer Thomas looks at the item and smiles, a transmitter, a bug, "Yes sir." The two men head off to find the communications tent. "Lt, find me when you're done, we will be in the UN Command tent." says Captain Spear.

"Aye, aye Skipper." replies Lt. Block.

The Master Chief stops in front of John, "You coming?" John jumps to his feet and grabs his gear.

"But he didn't," John starts to say but is interrupted.

"You forget why we are here; you hold the biggest coin at the table. You are on top of his chain of command; you are pretty much attached to our hips. Where we go, you go." And the two men exit down the ramp.

The Captain is speaking to two UN peacekeepers, they point off in a direction of some tents. Capt. Spear motions, "On me." The three men join Capt. Spear as they follow the two UN peacekeepers.

The men reach a large tent with a truck parked outside of it. It is dimly illuminated by the pole lights located throughout the complex. Chief Carison looks in back of the truck as he walks past it. He notices a large amount of what looks to be dried blood. There are ropes tied to the railings of the truck, and what looks to be a multicam jacket in the corner of the truck bed.

Chief Carison with the Stoner in hand jumps up on the truck's bed. The others are surprised by his move. Chief Carison walks over and picks up the jacket, smells it, "It's Mac's, he is or was here."

"And how do you know this is Mac's?" asks Capt. Spear.

"Pickles", says Chief Carison. The three men look puzzled at each other.

"Pickles?" says John puzzled.

"Mac loves pickles, Sandy used to give him hell about it. She called him pickle boy to tease him."

Chief Carison is reminiscing, thinking about the time he spent with his Dad when he was a boy.

"Who is Sandy?" asks Shane.

"She's Dad's," Chief Carison realizes he's letting his guard down and regroups, "Mac's girlfriend. Fiancé? I don't know, it has been a while, probably ten or twelve years now since I spent time with them."

Sgt Carison tosses the jacket to John. John catches the jacket and checks the left sleeve. There is a hole just where it should be if it was Mac's. John smells it before he hands it to Capt. Spear, "It's his." John sticks his finger out the hole where Mac took an AK round in his upper arm, "This is right where he took a round in our first fire fight." The Captain looks at the two UN peacekeepers that turn and open the doors to the tent. The four men enter the tent.

Once the men are inside the tent they are greeted with, "I am Captain Andre Mihailov. What is it I can do for the United States Navy?"

Captain Spear steps forward, "I am Captain Spear, I was told General Tarasovi was in charge of this UN base, I'd like to speak to him."

Captain Mihailov looks disturbed, "I regret to inform you that the General had an accident and is no longer with us. I have assumed command until the United Nations replaces me."

There is a knock on the door and in steps Lt. Block. Captain Spear turns, nods to the Lt. and looks at his men, then back to the UN Captain, "Fair enough, Captain, here is the message I was sent to tell him. Captain Spear's attitude and demeanor changes, "We have been sent to recover an American, an American I believe you have or had in your control. An American who probably caused an accident, or two." Capt. Spear moves closer to the UN Captain, "An American who for your sake better not be harmed, because when we find him, and we will find him, if he is harmed in any way I will personally find you and you will have an accident. Do you understand me Captain!"

"I know nothing of your American Soldier. I will not be threatened by you or the United States Navy. I will take this up with my UN superiors." states the Captain Mihailov, as he moves to his desk.

"We are done here," says Captain Spear and motions for the men to exit the tent. As they reach the door, Capt Spear stops and turns back toward the UN Captain. "We never said he was a soldier." The look of dread on Mihailov's face showed fear. "We will remain in the camp until we are satisfied he is not here." The men exit the tent.

★★★★★★★★★★★★★★★

It is dark and the moon is nowhere to be found. The landscape in front of him is mostly a void of darkness. Mac is moving slowly through the woods. He is about ten feet from the edge of the woods, he struggles with the lack of illumination from the moon as he studies the open ground in front of him. He can make out what looks to be a gravel road that is running East to West. Mac stays in the tree line and follows the road to the West until the road stops at a crude bridge. The ground slopes downward toward what he believes is a stream or river as he can hear the rush of water in front of him. Mac slowly moves down the slope as he looks for a place to rest. Mac finds a fallen tree he can shimmy under for cover. He places the two weapons next to him as he curls into a ball and falls asleep. Mac's mind drifts into a deep sleep, it has been days since he has been able to rest. He is dreaming about trucks or humvee's, the sounds of a river, kids playing.

The sun is coming over the tree tops. A young woman and young man venture down the hill toward the stream carrying two baskets of laundry. They break out the items and start washing the clothes in the stream. They hear trucks in the distance. Two Humvee's drive down the gravel road and pass by the young woman and man. They quickly try and gather up their clothes. They think they are okay, they haven't been seen, but then the

Humvee's screech to a stop and four soldiers exit the vehicles.

Two of the soldiers head down the hill to the man and woman. The other two soldiers stand near their vehicles. One of the soldiers grab the woman, and starts to pull her up the hill toward the vehicles. She is screaming, the other soldier is between the young man and the woman, he is pushing the young man away, they are both yelling at each other.

CHAPTER 11

Out of the fire, into...

Mac is still in a deep dream. There is a Marine in dress blues standing over him, yelling at him, Mac turns his head and looks dead in the Marine's eyes.

"Can't you hear them, Sergeant! Their cries for help? Are you just gonna lay there and let them die!"

Mac is confused, "No Gunny, but..."
"DON'T JUST LAY THERE THEY NEED YOUR HELP!"

Mac is startled awake by his dream. He can't believe the sun is up. Mac tries to look around struggling to acclimate to but the daylight. He can hear screams and yelling as he finds the source. Mac grabs his two weapons and heads up the embankment towards the bridge. At the top of the embankment, he steps on to the gravel road, and looks down the road to the East. He can't see much, mostly shaded objects as the sun is pretty much directly behind him. Mac checks both pistols, one is a Sig Sauer P-226, the other a Russian, MP-446 Viking. Mac Keeps the Sig in hand and places the MP in his waist band.

Mac starts walking toward the screams. He is about forty yards from the vehicles and can see everything illuminated by the sun. One soldier has dragged the woman almost to the top of the hill to the vehicles. The other is following them up the hill. The young man is still trying to get to the woman when the soldier stops, pulls his sidearm out of the holster, and points it at him. The young man raises his hands in front of him and continues to yell. The soldier fires the gun once and the young man falls backward to the ground. The soldier steps toward the young man and points the gun at the injured man.

Mac knows what is going to happen if he doesn't act. He quickly calculates his options. Mac knows he could slide back into the shadows and be safe, but he knows it isn't an option for him. He knows he would rather give his life trying to help or save someone, even if he doesn't know them. He knows this is going to turn out bad for him, but he doesn't care. Mac walks toward the soldiers and shouts loud enough for everyone to hear, "YAY THOUGH I WALK THROUGH THE SHADOW OF THE VALLEY OF DEATH, Mac pauses, I

SHALL FEAR NO EVIL...FOR I AM THE BIGGEST, BADDEST, MEANEST MOTHER FUCKER IN THE VALLEY!"

The soldier standing above the young man turns his attention away and searches for the voice. The other soldiers are also looking to see where the voice came from, yet all they can see is the bright sun.

The soldier pulling the woman disregards the voice and continues to pull the woman to the vehicles. "I WILL ONLY TELL YOU ONCE TO LET HER GO!" Mac stops about twenty-five yards from the vehicles and sets up in a firing stance. The pistol pointed toward the soldiers, Mac is relaxed, the sights are aligned on the soldier holding the woman's arm. The soldiers look around a second time, searching for the source of the voice. Then one of the soldiers sees an outline of a man in the sun and starts to point at him when CRACK, CRACK pierces the silence. The man holding the woman's arms looks at her and releases his grip and falls backward to the ground.

Mac makes slow precise movements as he moves forward and acquires a new target. The two soldiers by the vehicles aren't holding any weapons, but the man down the hill raises his pistol toward Mac and begins firing randomly. Mac takes aim, the sights are on the soldiers shoulder line, and he slowly squeezes the trigger, CRACK. The recoil is absorbed by his arms. Mac holds the squeeze on the trigger and slowly releases it until he feels the trigger resetting. Then, a second CRACK only seconds after the first. The second soldier falls backward to the ground, his arms spread out wide and the pistol still in the right hand. Mac turns his attention to the other two soldiers as they have retrieved rifles from the vehicles. Mac draws the second handgun with his left hand. Armed with two pistols, Mac moves toward the front of the vehicles as the other two soldiers have taken up positions behind them.

The soldiers are blindly firing bursts from behind the vehicles, spraying rounds up the road. Mac can see they are both on the same side of the vehicles. Mac fires toward them to keep their heads down and to keep them shooting in that particular direction. The two soldiers stick their guns out and fire. Mac does this one more time as he has reaches the front of the first Humvee.

When the soldiers stick their weapons out again, Mac moves to the other side of the vehicles and approaches the soldiers. One soldier shouts to the other and starts to reload his rifle. Mac steps out from behind the Humvee, the soldier sees the movement and turns toward it. All he sees is the flash of the pistol. The second soldier starts to shoot wildly into the Humvee between him and Mac. Mac ducks down, using the engine block as cover. The soldier stops firing. Mac hears a different weapon report over and over. Mac slowly looks over to see the young woman holding a pistol; it is empty and locked open. Mac lowers his weapons, steps out as he says, "I'm not here to hurt you. I want to help."

Mac puts his weapons away and walks over to the woman. He takes the pistol out of her hand. He pulls her close, "They aren't going to hurt you ever again."

Mac doesn't know if she understands him, "I need to check on the boy," Mac lets her go and heads down the hill to the young man.

The young man he is alive. Mac begins to administer first-aid to the boy. The girl runs down and kneels next to Mac. Mac looks at her, takes her hand and places it on the young man's shoulder wound. He pushes her hand down on the wound, "I need you to hold this like this." He releases her hand and runs back up to the Humvee's. He opens the door to the closest Humvee and searches inside for a few moments. He pulls out a medkit. As he gets out of the vehicle he sees a crowd of people standing at the edge of what looks to be a small village. They have been watching the events. Mac returns to the young man and starts dressing the wound.

As Mac is finishing patching up the young man he realizes he is surrounded by people. A group of men pick up the young man and take him to the village. Mac, uncomfortable with all these people around him, returns to the vehicles. The people are trying to shake his hand, pat him on the back, or just thank him for what he did. Mac tries to be gracious as he shakes hands and smiles. As they reach the vehicles the last person to thank him is the young woman. She hugs and kisses him on the cheek before she fades into the crowd.

Mac turns his attention to the dead UN soldiers. Mac searches through their clothing, collecting their ID's and anything else that might help him. Mac gathers up all their weapons and puts them in the second Humvee. Mac then gets the gas cans from the other vehicle, ensuring the Humvee he is going to use is full of fuel. Mac looks around at the dead UN soldiers, then the Humvee and then back at the dead men. Mac has put the third dead soldier into the back seat of the Humvee. He has strapped them all in with rope to make it look like they are passengers. Mac starts up the vehicle; he and his new passengers are on the move.

* * * * * * * * * * * * * * * *

The sun has been up for about an hour when the activity at the camp becomes frantic. The UN soldiers are running around loading vehicles and fueling helicopters. Petty Officer Thomas exits the rear of the Osprey and runs down the ramp toward a tent a few yards away. Petty Officer Thomas knocks on the door and waits for a response. "Enter", says a voice inside. Petty Officer Thomas enters the tent. Capt. Spear sits at a desk in the back of the room.

"Sir, we just intercepted a report of a lone man, who confronted four UN Soldiers, killing them in cold blood near a village about two hours from here.

The UN Commander here has authorized a response mission to locate him and bring him in dead or alive. They are scrambling two choppers, one MI-28 and H-92 Super Hawk Transport. In addition, they have two trucks they are loading with men and supplies."

Capt. Spear stands up, he is not very happy; he rants and raves about what he is going to do to the camp commander. He grabs his gear and heads out the door. Petty Officer Thomas is right behind him.

Capt. Spear rallies his men at the ramp of the Osprey.

"Here is what we are going to do. Lt. Block you and your team will secure this location. I need to know what they are doing or reporting. Once we have found Mac, you will regroup with us.

Just remember, you are the difference in us locating Mac before they do. In the case that they find him first, I will need you to secure the camp and take command of it. Use of force is authorized!"

* * * * * * * * * * * * * * *

Mac has been driving for about two hours, as the Humvee crests a small hill, he can see a Humvee blocking the road, four men standing around it. Mac knows if he stops or changes direction they will radio in and the chase would be on, but he also knows there is no way to avoid a fight once they see him and his passengers.

"Well boys, looks like we are going to have a fight on our hands. All we can hope is my trigger is faster and more accurate than they are."

He places an AK on the lap of the 'passenger.' Mac places magazines between the leg and the seat for easy access, and has two handguns on his lap. Mac studies the four UN soldiers near the Humvee blocking the road. One soldier is leaning up against the back of the Humvee, his weapon is hanging from his shoulder; another soldier is standing at the front of the vehicle with his right foot on the bumper, leaning on his leg, his weapon in hand, but not at the ready; two soldiers concern Mac, both standing with their weapons at the ready. None of the soldiers look to be wearing body armor. Mac stops his Humvee about ten feet from the blocking Humvee. He doesn't put the vehicle in park; he may need to make a fast getaway.

One of the soldiers starts to approach Mac, the other soldier examining the 'passenger.'

Mac's left arm is sitting on the door, his elbow in the open window, a pistol in his hand. Mac has another handgun in his right hand; it is held low, ready to go if needed. As the soldier gets close to the window Mac moves his left arm off the door and raises his left hand up. The soldier reaches Mac's door he leans down and looks in the window; he looks down the barrel of a gun. He looks at Mac, then looks around inside the vehicle. He sees three dead men.

Mac speaks softly to the soldier, "You can walk away, and no one has to die today."

The soldier turns his head ever so slightly and looks at the other standing man. The look in his eyes is that of horror. The second standing soldier sees the look in his partner's eyes and starts to walk toward the Humvee. The soldier looks back at Mac with fear in his eyes, he tries to speak but can't get any words out.

Mac looks at him then to the other soldier who is now approaching the front of the Humvee.

"You had a choice, you picked wrong." The handgun in his right hand fires first. CRACK, CRACK, CRACK. The soldier standing next to Mac takes three rounds in his chest; his body jerks and falls to the ground. Mac fires the handgun in his left hand at the approaching soldier, CRACK, CRACK, CRACK, CRACK. The windshield of the Humvee shatters as the rounds punch holes in it.

Mac can't tell if he hit the soldier due to the shattered windshield. Both handguns come to bear on the other two soldiers who are taken totally by surprise. The two soldiers look at their two comrades now lying dead on the ground. They scramble for cover as rounds are striking all around them. Mac fires at the two soldiers until both weapons lock open. Mac drops the two empty weapons and picks up the AK from the lap of his dead 'Passenger.' Mac fires the AK, its projectiles hurl toward the two soldiers scrambling for cover on the other side of the Humvee till it was empty.

Mac drops the empty magazine, reloads, and puts the barrel of the weapon on the dash. Mac he pushes the gas pedal to the floor. The vehicle lunges forward.

It hits a bump as it moves forward, Mac has the AK in his right hand and is firing short bursts, and is steering with his left. He again pushes the pedal to the floor and the vehicle accelerates again, but Mac is slow to turn the wheel as he is trying to aim the AK. His Humvee strikes the rear end of the UN Humvee, moving it a couple of feet, and Mac keeps driving.

The soldier who took cover near the rear of the vehicle is thrown when the vehicles collide and lands on the ground about two feet away from the weapon he dropped. All the soldier can do is to get small, become the ground, as there is nothing to hide behind. As Mac passes the rear of the UN Humvee he moves the AK to the passenger window, emptying the magazine, the rounds are striking all around the Humvee.

The other UN soldier is hunkered down behind the front end trying to avoid being hit by incoming rounds. Mac's Humvee speeds off. The two soldiers grab their weapons and start firing at the back of the Humvee. Mac can hear the rounds striking the Humvee as he drives off.

Mac drives down a dirt road and he notices the Humvee is slowing down. He looks to the gauges and realizes the fuel tank is on empty, the Humvee's engine cuts out and rolls to a stop. Mac, cussing like a drunken sailor, exits the Humvee. He walks to the back of the vehicle to see if any of the fuel cans have fuel. All the cans have holes in them, empty. Mac scans the surrounding landscape for a place to hide, plan his next move. As he retrieves the gear and weapons from inside the Humvee he hears a vehicle approaching. Mac stands up and looks behind him to see a Humvee, approximately one hundred yards away, bearing down on his position. Mac pulls two grenades from the dead UN soldier's web gear and moves away from the vehicle, using it as cover.

The driver and passenger in the Humvee scan the area as they approach the Humvee stopped in the road. They haven't seen Mac, but they know he has to be close; they ready their weapons.

Mac pulls the two pins and tosses the grenades under the front of his vehicle and takes off running. The grenades explode under the Humvee, causing a great fireball and smoke plume. Mac uses the explosion as a distraction as he heads up a small hill to a rocky area in some trees for cover.

The driver of the Humvee slams on the breaks as the vehicle in front of him explodes in a ball of fire. Both men exit their vehicle and take cover searching the surroundings through the billowing black smoke, unable to locate him.

Mac reaches the rocks and dives over them. He lays there for a few moments listening for movement. Mac slowly rolls to his hands and knees and looks for an opening to try and see what is happening back at the vehicles.

Mac watches as the two UN soldiers get to their feet with weapons ready and move toward the burning Humvee. It looks as if they didn't see where he ran to. Mac sits back on his haunches and grabs an H&K 93, taken from one of the dead UN soldiers

Humvee, slightly pulls back on the charging handle to make sure it has a round in the chamber. He slowly rises up above the rocks to get a visual on the two hostiles. Their attention is on the area around the burning Humvee. Mac brings the rifle up onto the rock to steady his aim. The two men are about fifty yards away. One man on either side of the burning vehicle. Mac's choice is easy as he puts the sights on the man's chest. The man turns to his left, giving a full-chest view to Mac. Mac exhales slightly and holds his breath as he squeezes the trigger. 'Crack' and the rifle kicks slightly. Mac watches the man fall to the ground, and then he tries to acquire the second man. The second man has crouched behind the burning Humvee and scans the hill side looking for the shooter. He fires randomly into the hillside and he runs back to their Humvee. Mac takes aim, leading the man slightly as he pulls the trigger again, the CRACK echoes as the second man falls to the ground.

As Mac gathers up his weapons and gear he hears the sound of an aircraft approaching, not the sound of a helicopter, but a fixed prop. Mac drops the gear, grabs the H&K 93 and gets as close to the rocks as he can for cover. Mac scans the horizon for the aircraft.

****

As the Osprey approaches the area, Tony and John are searching for any signs of Mac. They can see the billowing smoke from two vehicles and two bodies nearby. They circle one more time before starting the transition to a rotary wing for landing.

CHAPTER 12

Incoming

Out of the sun comes a familiar site to Mac, an Osprey, and it can only be his friends coming to find him. Mac gathers up his stuff and starts down the hill toward the Osprey as it lands.

The ramp of the Osprey opens, Mac can see a group of men standing on it, hollering at him. Mac's spirits are at their highest since the mission began, he had given up on being rescued and believed he would die here.

As the Osprey settles onto the ground, the men move down the ramp toward Mac. Mac sees John and his old friend Shane along with numerous men he doesn't know. These new men take his gear and head back into the Osprey. John extends his hand to Mac, "I told you we'd be back for you."

Mac shakes his friend's hand. Shane extends his also, but Mac grabs him and pulls him toward him and pats him on the back, "Thanks for coming to help." Mac goes quiet; tears start to build up in his eyes as he sees his son.

As John and Shane step away, Chief Carison smiling, holds up the Stoner, "Did you lose something old man?" The two men walk toward each other; Sgt Carison tosses the Stoner to John as he and Mac embrace.

"I didn't expect to see you here." says Mac.

"You were in trouble, I wouldn't be anywhere else." says Chief Carison.

* * * * * * * * * * * * * * *

On approach are a UN Mi-28 attack helicopter and two H-92 SuperHawk transport helicopters. The pilot of the Mi-28 is on its approach to the area when they realize that there is an aircraft on the ground, "Command, we have unknown aircraft and personnel on the ground in the area we lost contact with the check point vehicle."

"Command to attack helicopter, this is a kill, no capture mission are we clear."

"Clear" replies the pilot.

* * * * * * * * * * * * * * *

Capt. Spear stands at the top of the

ramp, "I hate to break up this happy reunion, but we have hostile choppers inbound, we got to move now." The four men rush up the ramp into the Osprey as it jumps off the ground.

"Missiles inbound, this is going to be rough, HANG ON!" shouts Tony, "Captain Spear, I need you up here now."

Capt. Spear rushes to the cock-pit and climbs in a seat. "Get on the radio and get a hold of the Ronald Reagan."

Capt. Spear grabs the mic and changes the frequency, "Ronald Reagan, Ronald Reagan, this is JoyRide, MayDay! MayDay! MayDay! We are taking fire from a UN Havoc." He keeps repeating the message.

Tony puts all the rpm's into the engines to quickly gain altitude. The missiles from the UN Mi-28 strike the ground where the Osprey was; the explosion is fiery bright and the Osprey bounces around a bit.

The UN pilot believes he has a kill and starts to head back toward his base when his navigator/weapons officer advises they missed. The pilot looks back toward the Osprey and seeing it rising off the ground he takes a pot shot at it with his 30mm cannon the shot is wild, but catches the port side of the cockpit and engine. There is a small explosion and the engine flames out. The Osprey loses altitude.

Mac was standing next to the cock-pit when the windshield explodes inward. He can feel the rush of air, wetness on his face and the smell of death all around. He realizes he is sitting against two dead SEALs. The Osprey is at an awkward angle, and he can see Tony struggling to keep it airborne. Mac looks around and the men are all on the starboard side of the plane. There is blood and remains splattered everywhere, as Mac climbs into the cockpit and sees what is left of Capt. Spear in the co-pilots chair. The windshield is half-gone and as MAC looks out there is a helicopter circling back at them and two transport helicopters headed at them.

Mac yells he needs a weapon, and John hands him the Stoner. Mac puts the barrel out the window and tries to get a bead on the chopper circling back around. Mac remembers the Havoc is heavily armored and his .223 round wouldn't scratch the paint. Mac turns his attention to the lead H-92, and he squeezes the trigger and let's fly a stream of lead.

The Osprey is going down fast, and will be even faster if the Havoc can get a shot. "We are going to hit hard guys, prepare for impact." hollers Tony as he starts to open the exit ramp. The Havoc has almost made its full turn and is lining up for the kill; he brings the 30mm cannon to bear, his finger on the trigger to the 80mm rockets. Mac continues to fire at the cockpit windshield of the H-92.

The pilot of the H-92 is startled by the first rounds that strike the cockpit. He doesn't think much of it as he knows the attack helicopter is on its approach to finish off the aircraft. The rounds from the Osprey are tearing up the cockpit. The glass starts to shatter, then rounds begin to penetrate. The pilot panics and jerks the joy stick to the right in an attempt to escape the flurry of lead.

The H-92's erratic turn takes its rotor's into the tail rotor of the Mi-28 just as it begins to fire. The Mi-28 jerks violently and begins to spin out of control, the 30mm cannon fires randomly as it spins, the rockets fire harmlessly into the air. The Mi-28 spins out of control into the ground and explodes. The H-92 having lost part of its rotors continues its arch to the right and also explodes as it strikes the ground.

The Osprey falls to the ground and comes apart from impact, there are some small fires, but the Osprey doesn't explode. John sees the ramp door is halfway open and directs MC Myers and Chief Carison to move the injured out of the dead ship to safety. Mac grabs Tony and helps him out of the cockpit. Tony reaches back inside the cockpit and grabs his flight bag and they head out of the plane.

Once all the men are safe they take a head count: three men KIA, two SEALs injured, no life threatening injuries.

"Capt. Spear is still in the co-pilots seat, at least what's left of him and I know at least two of your SEALs are in there also." states Mac.

Tony wipes the blood and matter from his face, "The first rounds from the Havocs 30mm ripped through the windshield, one sec he was there calling for help and then he was gone. He wasn't more than two feet from me. That's what must have gotten the others before it took out the engine."

"What we have to do now is find some cover. We are going to have to move with the wounded as fast as we can. Take a quick inventory of what we have, gather up everything we can carry." says MC Myers.

While the SEALs are gathering useful equipment and gear, Mac heads over to the Humvee's, checks for fuel. Mac starts the engine and pulls up near the group, "Anyone need a taxi?" jokes Mac. The men load up the Humvee with the wounded and equipment and head south.

* * * * * * * * * * * * * * *

On board the Ronald Reagan, the radio operator picks up a faint signal but can't understand it. He plays back the recording and amplifies it to see if he can make it out. "Ronald Reagan, Ronald Reagan, this is JoyRide Mayday! Mayday! Mayday! We are taking fire from a UN Havoc. "Ronald Reagan, Ronald Reagan, this is JoyRide Mayday! Mayday! Mayday! We are taking fire from a UN Havoc." Then the message stops.

"XO, you are going to need to hear this." says the radio operator.

The XO walks over and puts on the head set. His eyes get wide as he hears the message. He removes the headset, "Get the Skipper, NOW!" One of the crew takes off to the Captains quarters.

* * * * * * * * * * * * * * *

The SecNav stands behind a desk on the phone, "I understand, Captain, you have complete authority to do whatever is necessary to get our boys out. I will get you an Emergency Action Message (EAM) with my authorization within the hour; this is an active combat mission. I, and only I, have Command and Control of this operation. If you do not get the following code word; **FIREFLY**, you will treat any message as hostile and not authentic. Do you understand?" there is a pause. "Good. Bring our boys home, Captain."

The SecNav hangs up the phone and pushes a button on his desk, "Michelle, I need you in here to take down a message." The door opens and in walks a young lady with her note pad.

* * * * * * * * * * * * * * * *

On the bridge of the USS Ronald Reagan, the Captain turns to his crew, "Sound General Quarters, this is not a drill, I need all Command Officers from the battle group in my Ready Room."

"Also contact the UN Command in Georgia and advise them their airspace is now a No-Fly-Zone. I also need a secure line to the Prime Minister of Turkey. I'll take it in my ready room." says the Captain walking off the bridge.

The General Quarters alarm sounds on the USS Ronald Reagan and across the battle group. Men scramble to their combat stations. Helicopters are coming and going from the battle group and the USS Ronald Reagan.

In the Captains ready room sit the command officers. Captain Martin is laying out the orders and wishes from the SecNav and what he has planned. The officers stand at attention when Captain Martin leaves the ready room. The men then look to each other and start talking.

Activity across the fleet is in full stride. Marines in full combat gear are headed to the armory where they are handed their assigned weapon and they head off to their designated helicopter. The Officers start returning to their ships.

Captain Martin stands on the bridge surveying the men and women who are working there. Captain Martin picks up the hand set and instructs his radio operator to broadcast both ship and fleet wide:

"This is Captain Martin, I have met with all the Fleet Officers, and I have told them what I am about to tell every member of this fleet. We are about to go into combat, for most of you that means you will do your jobs here on your ships, for others that means you will board the helicopters and fly off to face an enemy that is supposed to be our ally, but an unknown contingent has its own loyalties. In a nut shell, they are moving nuclear materials from Russia to North Korea and we had men on the ground that recovered the evidence we need to prove this. We have men on the ground in harm's way. This mission is strictly voluntary. The SecNav advised this course of action will END his career. He knows this and accepts it. I know that this could very well end mine. This is a choice each and every one of you must consider. Any officer, Seaman or Marine that wishes to stand down may do so. Merely get up from your station and return to your bunk. But, I for one will not leave our men on the field, not on my watch!"

No one moves.

Across the fleet the men and women do not leave their posts, they give their commanding officers a thumbs up. The Marines preparing to board the helicopters stand at attention, "URah….SEMPER FI!" They load into their assigned helicopters. An assortment of AH-1W, Super Cobra's, CH-46, Sea Knight helicopter, and CH-53 Sea Stallion helicopters sit on the flight deck and lifting off of the USS Iwo Jima and the USS Peleliu.

★★★★★★★★★★★★★★★

The SecNav sits at his desk when his assistant, Michelle, enters the room, "I just got a call from the White House." The SecNav grins. "Hum, really. Let me guess, I've been summoned."

Michelle smiles, "Yes Sir, you are to report to the Oval Office at 0800 tomorrow morning."

The SecNav stands up, "Well, I guess we need to get ready. Have you ever been to the White House?"

"No Sir, I have not."

"Well, I want you in the room when we get there. Even if he tells you to leave you are not to go, is that understood?"

"Yes Sir," says Michelle as she leaves the room.

The SecNav picks up his phone and dials a number, he waits a few moments, "I need to speak to Bruce," says Pepper into the phone,

"I need you at a meeting in the morning at the White House." He pauses for a few moments as he listens, "Yeah I'm sure it's going to be just like you said, so, 0800 and bring your copies." Pepper listens, then, "CYA Bruce, CYA." And Pepper hangs up.

* * * * * * * * * * * * * * * *

The room is dark as Captain Mihailov rolls over and turns on the lamp next to his bed. It takes a moment for him to realize there is a man sitting in a chair a few feet away from him and he is startled and reaches for his service weapon.

"Looking for this?" says Lt. Block as he holds up the Russian's pistol.

"Ivan, Demitri," shouts Captain Mihailov. Nothing, The Captain looks around for his guards. "What are you doing in my quarters?" demands Mihailov.

"Don't worry about your guards, they have been, well, let's just say they have been relieved of their duties, and to be honest I have been sitting here for a while trying to decide what I was going to do. Honestly, I couldn't decide how I was going to do it. One to the head while you slept or to wake you up so you knew, then it all became clear."

The doors to the room open and two members of the SEAL Team and two well dressed men entered. "I think you know Comrade Uri and Comrade Tarasov." said Lt. Block.

Captain Mihailov has a pensive look on his face as he moves back against the wall. "So, I was gonna do the dirty work, but we, well, the Comrade's and I have come to an arrangement. We get their helicopter and they get you."

Lt. Block smiles and gets up and starts to walk away.

"I can provide you with any and all information regarding your friend and our internal operations, in exchange for your protection." says Captain Mihailov. With his back still toward Mihailov, "Unfortunately for you, we have everything we need; you see, your communications Officer kept quite detailed records and he has traded them for asylum, so you are of no use to us."

Lt. Block hands Comrade Uri Captain Mihailov's pistol.

"Although this arrangement isn't perfect, we can at least live with it." says Comrade Uri. Lt. Block and the other two Team members leave the room. Comrade Uri and Tarasov move toward Mihailov.

Once outside the tent, the men are met by Chief Jones, "We are all loaded on the chopper and ready to roll." states Chief Johnson. The four men head off to the helipad, get into the helicopter and it takes off.

As the helicopter rotors are spinning up, Tim looks at Lt. Bloc, shrugs his shoulders, "You know, we are in a Russian helicopter, it might be a good idea to make sure they know it's friendly. I think you need to make a call." and points to the radio.

Lt. Block adjusts the radio frequency, "Ronald Reagan, Ronald Reagan this is Bravo Actual, do you copy?"

There is only static. Lt. Block repeats, "Ronald Reagan, Ronald Reagan this is Bravo Actual do you copy?"

"Bravo Actual this is the Ronald Reagan, we copy. Need SitRep ASAP!"

"SitRep as follows, have needed doc's and one to verify. We have acquired a Russian bird, but need to make sure that bird's wings aren't clipped."

"We copy, Bravo Actual, your wings are clear to fly." "Copy, any other info you can provide?"

* * * * * * * * * * * * * * *

It's dark now, the Humvee has been driving for a couple of hours, when it starts to sputter and rolls to a stop.

"Well, gents, looks like we get to hoof it now." jokes John.

What's left of the team exits the vehicle, unloads the wounded and gear. They have lost their Captain and two of the SEALs, the group is down to ten from thirteen and two of those SEALs are injured. They distribute the gear and load the two wounded up on the back and shoulders of their teammates. The walking wounded start off on foot down the road as the others push the Humvee off the road and into the brush and follow.

The group hasn't been on the road for more than a few minutes when one of the men in the back of the group notices headlights coming up the road. Chief Mallow stops and takes a moment to process what he sees, "COVER NOW, incoming vehicles!"

Chief Mallow and the rest of the group scatter into the brush on both sides of the road.

The men have taken cover on both sides of the road and each one prepares for a fight they hope they can avoid. One vehicle passes by, and then another and another until eight trucks in total pass the group hidden in the brush. The men wait for about thirty minutes before coming out from cover. The men again prepare for their journey, they gather their gear and are about to move out when another set of headlights are coming up the road, this time they are closer when they are spotted. Chief Carison sees them and shouts out, "CONTACT REAR!"

* * * * * * * * * * * * * * *

The driver of the truck sees what he believes is a man standing in the middle of the road, he looks harder and distinguishes a group of men in the road.

"American soldiers, fire, fire, fire." The men in back of the truck raise their weapons and begin to fire down the road at the illuminated men in headlights.

Petty Officer Odhem, making sure the wounded men are safe first, doesn't heed the warning fast enough as the rounds from the truck rip through his body and strike the ground around him.

The team scatters to the sides of the road and bring their weapons to bear on the vehicle, and return fire. The teams' rounds are ripping through the cab of the truck, while the enemy's rounds are striking all around them.

Chief Mallow, the corpsman, rushes to Odhem's side to check his wounds. The Petty Officer Odhem's wounds are mortal but the Chief finds a pulse, Chief Mallow grabs Odhem by his combat harness with his left hand and starts to drag him to cover when he is hit in the left shoulder by gun fire. Mallow spins to the ground but gets back up, changes his grip to his right hand pulling the dying man to cover.

As they both lay there, wounded, not
knowing if they would live or die. Chief
Mallow opens his medkit and takes out a
syringe of morphine, and injects it into
Odhem's leg.

"Hang in there Petty Officer, you are
going to make it."

Odhem looks at Mallow, and holds up his
right hand. Odhem is coughing up blood.

Mallow grabs Odhem's hand.

Odhem, having a hard time talking.

"I've been where you are Chief, I know
better." Tears streak down Odhem's cheeks.

"Tell my wife I love her, and my son I'm
sorry, I won't--."

Mallow is having a hard time holding
his composure.

"Your gonna." Mallow stops talking as
Petty Officer Odhem dies in his arms.

"You have my promise friend." as he
closes Odhem's eyes and lowers his body to
the ground.

The enemy gun fire stops as the truck
rolls to a stop just off the road.

Mac starts to move forward, weapon at
the ready, "On me! Carison, right tree line,
John left!" The men take their positions and

advance toward the truck. As they reach the truck they check the dead and look for survivors. The truck would normally carry twenty men and two men in the cab, but only ten bodies were located. The others may have escaped into the darkness.

MC Myers shouts, "Check for anything useful and let's move out before they come back or radio the first group." The men gather up weapons, ammunition and all the explosives that they could find and return to the others.

Mac, MC Myers and John kneel next to Chief Mallow as Petty Officer Mitchell is tending to the Chiefs wounds. "Im good to go Master Chief." says Chief Mallow. Myers pats Mallow on the back as he starts to stand up, "That's good, Chief, cause I have a feeling we are gonna need yours and Mitchell's services again soon."

"It's going to be a bit tougher, especially with wounded, but we need to get off the road and move cross country," says Mac, turning to MC Myers, "I didn't mean to step on your toes and take charge, it's just a habit."

MC Myers puts his hand on Macs shoulder, "We have been friends a long time, and you guys have a lot more time in, well, let's just say I know you guys have been places and done things our SEAL Teams only read about. So with that said, you are senior, in more ways than one."

MC Myers starts laughing and walks away. Mac chuckles, "yeah, yeah."

Mac picks up his Stoner and checks the ammo box, then picks up his pack, "I'll take point."

MC Myers steps up, "I got point old man, hang back and try to keep up," as he walks past Mac and pats him on the shoulder. "Okay then, John take Petty Officer Jones, Mallow help Ensign Lake. Tony stay close to them and help them out if you can. Chief Mitchell, right flank and Chief Carison, the left. This old man will bring up the rear." The men gather everything up and head off into the dark of the night.

* * * * * * * * * * * * * * *

The men have been traveling all night and have stopped to rest at what they believe is the end of the treeline before a clearing. MC Myers is joined by Mac. MC Myers looks at his watch, then at Mac.

Mac motions and the rest of the men to gather around them, "Well, we have been on the move for longer than I care to remember. We have come so far, and we only have a little farther to go, but these last few miles will be the hardest and deadliest. We have a few hours of dark before dawn. Those trucks that passed us with all the soldiers are out there waiting to stop us. We must move fast, yet, quiet. Prepare yourself for what lies ahead; as this is going to be our toughest challenge yet."

The men disperse and prepare their gear. They are reloading and redistributing magazines, tying down anything that would make unwanted noises as they move. Once everyone was ready they reformed on Mac. Mac puts on his pack then grabs the Stoner 63a, "Alright guys, we have all been here before, you all know your jobs and assignments, we have come this far, I want us all to get home."

MC Myers pats Mac on the shoulder, "I still have point old friend!"

Mac bows slightly and moves his arm from inside to out. MC Myers chuckles and heads into the darkness, followed by the rest of the team. Mac is the last to fade into the darkness.

The men are moving at fairly good pace; they have been on the move for a couple of hours and are keeping an eye on the surroundings as they are becoming visible as the sun starts to rise. The team should have a slight advantage as the sun rises the higher ground will become visible before the shadowed ground in the valley.

CHAPTER 13

Fulfilling a promise

There is a knock on the door to the Oval Office. The Presidents Secretary opens the door. "They are here Mr. President." As they enter the room they can see the President sitting behind the desk with his back towards them. Michelle is the first to enter and is followed by the Secretary of the Navy and the Director of the CIA. Once in the room, the two men walk to the front of the desk. The President stands up and turns toward them as Michelle closes the door behind her and moves to the back of the room.

"Mr. President" says the SecNav as he extends his hand. The President shakes hands, "Pepper." "Mr. President," says the Director of the CIA as he also extends his right hand.

"Bruce," says the President as he shakes his hand.

"This won't take long gentlemen, Michelle, if you would excuse us. I need to speak with Pepper and Bruce."

The SecNav stands tall in front of the President, "She will stay at my request Mr. President."

The President looks irritated at the arrogance shown by the SecNav.

"Fine, have it your way. I have been getting calls for the last couple of days from the United Nations and the President of Russia. Everyone is up in arms about our military mobilization in Turkey and Georgia. Can you tell me what the hell is going on?"

"To be honest, Mr. President, you have been kept up to date on everything that has been going on in Georgia."

Pepper motions to Bruce, "The Director of the CIA and I have worked together to provide your office with daily reports since the CIA agents discovered there were barrel-sized canisters of enriched uranium being smuggled from Russia through Georgia to oil tankers bound for North Korea. But all the evidence we had is missing since those agents went dark. And, I'm guessing you don't remember authorizing the "civilian" recovery team we sent in to get the agents and the Intel back? -- Do you remember our conversation about the operation to get our people back when the recovery op fell apart?"

The President runs his hand through his hair as he looks down at the floor, "A lot has happened since those conversations Pepper, a lot that you are not aware of. Things that even the SecNav or the Director of the CIA are not privy to." The President turns his back to the two men and stares out the window.

"Exactly what has changed, Mr. President? Enriched uranium is still being shipped to North Korea; we still have men and women's lives at risk on the ground! Those agents have risked their lives to help keep this country safe. And, to top it off, we have sent men in to rescue those agents. But I have a feeling you're about to tell us that those lives are expendable for some greater good." says Bruce.

The President turns around and faces Pepper and Bruce, "It doesn't matter anymore, gentlemen, it's out of our hands. What does matter is that you recall those troops and have them stand down."

Pepper looks to Bruce then back to the President, "I take it you or the Joint Chiefs have attempted to recall the troops but have failed to do so."

The President is angry now, the veins in his neck are bulging and he points at Pepper,

"I am giving you a direct order to contact the Ronald Reagan and have them stand down and return to their ships, is that understood? Then I want your resignation on my desk before the end of business today!"

The SecNav smiles at the President, leans his hands on the edge of his desk, "I, we, have troops in the field, troops you authorized. I will not abandon them. I have watched as you and previous administrations have left our men behind to fend for themselves. US soldiers or US agents are expendable when deals have been made in some sleazy back room which would look bad to the voters if the truth were made public, like Bengazi. Well sir, I will not let another life fade into the darkness because I am ordered to by some elected pompous ass who has never served, or put his life on the line for this great country. You want my resignation? Well Sir, I want your resignation! But, I will not give you my resignation; if you want me gone then you will have to remove me. My first responsibility is to this country and to the men and women I serve. Before you would have the chance to do it I would provide to the press, this file."

Pepper takes the file from Bruce and drops it on the President's desk. "This, Sir, is a copy of a file. In this file is every report and memo I have at my disposal regarding this joint operation. I will not be forced to sacrifice anymore lives, Mr. President!"

The President leans in toward Pepper, "Are you trying to blackmail the President of the United States?"

Pepper stiffens and crosses his arms, "No, sir, I'm just doing what is right, saving those who WE put in harm's way."

The President is livid. He starts to say something and stops on multiple occasions, speechless. Finally the President bellows two words, "GET OUT!"

Bruce and Pepper turn around to leave, Michelle holds the door for them. The President scowls at Michelle as the two men exit the room and she closes the door behind her.

* * * * * * * * * * * * * * * *

Mac hears something behind him, and turns his attention toward the noise. Mac stops, kneels down and brings his Stoner to bear on the ground from which they had just came. The rest of the team has continued moving forward and are unaware Mac has stopped. The team is about twenty yards away when Chief Carison glances behind him and realizes that Mac isn't there.

Chief Carison makes a clicking noise with his mouth to try and get the rest of the team's attention. Tony hears the clicking, looks back to see Chief Carison holding up his closed fist, indicating he wanted the team to stop. Tony makes a slight, quiet whistle towards MC Myers. MC Myers hears the noise and looks back to see the rest of the Team stopped. He moves back to contact Chief Carison, "Mac isn't in sight, I'm not sure where he went?" says Chief Carison.

As Chief Carison and MC Myers are scan the ground behind them, Chief Mitchell puts his right hand on MC Myers shoulder to get his attention, with his left arm he points to their left, towards the higher ground. The sun is high enough in the sky it has illuminated the hillside and hundreds of soldiers. Fortunately for the Team they are still in the shadows, but not for much longer.

MC Myers looks around for any escape or cover options. There is a tree line, but it's at least one hundred yards away. The only other option is a small depression with some rocks as cover, "It's go time men, I don't know Mac's status, and, right now, it's not our problem." MC Myers points to a grouping of rocks about thirty yards to the left of them, "That is our stand, get there and get ready for the fight of your life!"

The team gets ready to move when they hear gunfire in Mac's last known location.

"MOVE NOW!" shouts MC Myers. The team is off and running, with the exception of Chief Carison who is looking toward the gunfire.

"I know you're worried about Mac, but right now Drew, you have men depending on you. Move your ass!" says MC Myers.

Chief Carison, while still looking for Mac, "Aye, Aye, Master Chief!" They are both up and running toward the rest of the team.

Once they reach the safety of cover MC Myers turns to his men, "Okay, guys, this is it. Don't waste your ammo. As it is, we are low, pick and choose your targets, be smart, ammo conservation." The Team has taken cover behind the rocks and starts to engage the UN Soldiers.

****

It is getting lighter and easier to make out the landscape as Mac scans the area. Right in front of him is a group of about ten men moving quickly toward him. Mac shoulders his Stoner, takes aim at the lead man and pulls the trigger. The Stoner does what it was designed to do, throw a wall of lead at its target in an effective killing manner. Mac picks and chooses his targets as they get closer to him, they fall one by one. The oncoming group of men has run into a sledge hammer. The group is cut down before they realize what has happened. Mac scans the area again as he removes the ammo box from his Stoner and replaces it with a full box. Mac turns his attention to where the rest of the team was supposed to be.

* * * * * * * * * * * * * * * *

On the high ground are hundreds of UN
Soldiers, they are searching the shadowy
landscape below them looking for any sign of
the men they have been sent to kill.
Automatic gunfire gets their attention, but
they can't see anything, just muzzle flashes.
The UN Soldiers just start firing blindly
down into the shadows.

Mac turned around and moves in the
direction of the team. He hears new gunfire
off to his right; he looks up the hillside he
can see hundreds of soldiers and hundreds of
muzzle flashes. Mac looks for cover and sees
muzzle flashes coming from about thirty yards
away. He knows it is the rest of the team.
Mac starts heading toward the rest of the
team, and feels multiple thumps in his right
side and goes spinning to the ground.

* * * * * * * * * * * * * * * *

Inside the helicopters cockpit, "Lt, do
you see that at your eight o'clock?" asks
Tim.

Lt. Block scans the area at his eight o'clock and can see tracer rounds going in multiple directions, "Can we get a closer look? I'd bet that's our boys!" Lt. Block's reply really isn't a question, more of a statement.

Tim heads the helicopter in the direction of the tracers. Lt. Block presses his mic, "Ronald Reagan, Ronald Reagan, this is Bravo Actual, do you copy."

There is a brief moment of static, then, "Bravo Actual, this is Ronald Reagan, we copy."

"Be advised, we believe we have found JoyRide, I say again, we believe we have located JoyRide."

"Bravo Actual, we copy last. Do you have JoyRide now?" asks the Ronald Reagan.

"Negative, Ronald Reagan, have visual on a firefight, going to investigate. Copy our current coordinates and we will advise, over." says Lt. Block.

"Roger, Bravo Actual, our birds are out of the nest, their feet are dry, awaiting orders. We will get them up and moving." replies the Ronald Reagan's radio operator.

* * * * * * * * * * * * * * * *

Sitting idle on an airfield somewhere in
northern Turkey, are thirty helicopters with
three hundred plus men waiting, when they get
the order to mount up. The men scramble to
load. The blades on the helicopters start to
spin until they are rotating at maximum
velocity for takeoff. The tall grass and
weeds are pressed against the ground as they
leave the ground.

* * * * * * * * * * * * * * * *

The helicopter is now just above the
tree tops as it buzzes between the UN Troops
and the missing SEAL Team. "That's our boys
down there." says Tim as he starts to circle
around for another pass.

Lt. Block gets on his coms. "Since this
is a Russian diplomatic helicopter, the UN
guys must think we are with them. We can set
down far enough away from their lines and
work our way back to them and see if we can
take them by surprise."

Tim gives him the thumbs up and looks
for an LZ nearby. The rest of the SEAL Team

check their gear and ready themselves for action.

* * * * * * * * * * * * * * *

Chief Carison is returning fire at the UN Soldier's when movement on his right catches his attention. He glances to his right to see Mac moving toward them, and then Mac spins and lies motionless on the ground.

Chief Carison cries out, "Dad," and starts to leave his cover to help Mac. MC Myers grabs him by the duty belt stopping him; "You can't help him right now. We need to keep them busy so he has a chance."

Sgt Carison looks at MC Myers, "With all due respect, Master Chief, that's my father lying out there, and unless you are giving me a direct order not to go and get him, - "

"No, Sgt., no order, you have to do what you have to do."

"Step it up men, we have a man down, keep'em busy!" shouts the Master Chief.

The rest of the Team increases their fire, picking and choosing more rapidly. Chief Carison is out from behind his cover moving fast and low to the ground. He slides

on his knees next to Mac and checks for a
pulse.

"Damn, son, I thought you were smarter
than that!" says Mac as he lies there.

"I got my smarts from you!" jokes
Sgt.Carison.

"Well, I think the vest took most of the
damage, and since you're here, get me up and
back in the fight!" says Mac.

As rounds land all around them, Chief
Carison throws his weapon over his shoulder
and grabs Mac's vest and they both get to
their feet. Mac with his Stoner and Chief
Carison with his M4 start to head toward the
rest of the team.

Mac stops them and points up the hill,
"If I'm going out, its going to be fighting,
not running." states Mac.

Sgt Carison shrugs his shoulders, "I'm
right behind you."

Both men move up the hill as fast as
they can. Chief Carison is on his coms,
"Master Chief, this is Carison, we are
attempting to flank, do you copy? I say
again, this is Carison, we are attempting to
flank, do you copy?" there is static, then
"copy attempting to flank, over."

****

The helicopter is hovering just feet from the ground as the rest of the SEAL Team jumps to the ground. Lt. Block holds for a moment as he tries to make out a coms transmission. Then he follows his men. Once on the ground they move to a defensive position as the helicopter moves away. Once the helicopter is out of view, Lt. Block signals his team to move. Lt. Block activates his coms, "We are going to move rickity quick to engage, be advised, we have friendly's moving in our direction from the bottom of the hill. Be sure of your targets".

The men move toward the threat on the opposite side of the hill. Once the Team crests the top of the hill, they can see a couple of hundred hostiles lining the roadway. "Alpha, this is Bravo Actual, Alpha this is Bravo Actual, do you copy?" says Lt. Block on his coms.

A few moments go by, "Copy Lt., this is Myers, we are getting our asses handed to us down here, taking massive fire, not sure how long we can hold out."

The hostile's attention is focused on the rest of their team down in the valley and they do not seem concerned about anything else.

Lt. Block signals for the men to spread out and position themselves. Once in position the SEALs start picking off targets from the back working forward, they continue to do this as they move down the roadway.

* * * * * * * * * * * * * * *

One of the UN soldiers catches a comrade falling toward him out of the corner of his eye. The soldier looks toward him as the body falls at his feet. He looks up to see soldiers moving toward him and swings his weapon in their direction and starts yelling, "Americans! Americans!" He fires at the SEALs. Some of the soldiers closest to him hear his warnings and also look toward the threat. They realize the deadliest threat is right in front of them. They bring their weapons to bear on the new targets and begin to fire.

Ensign, "Shwabby", Shwarburg is on point. He clicks his mic, "The jig is up

boys!" Shwabby drops his M-4 and it falls to his side hanging by
the combat harness and pulls a grenade out of his web gear, pulls the pin out and throws it into the group that has turned their attention to them, "Frag out!" Shwabby reaches down with his right hand grabbing the pistol grip of his M4, lifts the weapon back into firing position, and goes back to firing as the grenade explodes in the middle of the group of men sending them and parts of them aloft.

* * * * * * * * * * * * * * *

The helicopter circles out wide from where the SEALs were dropped off. Tony keys up the mic, "Ronald Reagan, Ronald Reagan, this is Joyride, do you copy?" There is a short period of static.

"Joyride, this is Ronald Reagan, we copy you".

"Roger, Ronald Reagan, sit rep as follows: Alpha engaged by unknown number of hostiles and are pinned down. Bravo is on ground moving to engage. We need support ASAP, over!"

"Roger, Joyride, fast birds in the air, support en route, over."

"Copy Ronald Reagan, will do what we can till support arrives." says Tony.

* * * * * * * * * * * * * * * *

Mac and Chief Carison have moved to the top of the hill and can see the road with the UN soldiers on it. Mac turns to his Son, "We are going to cross over the road to get the high ground, don't stop. No matter what."

Chief Carison interrupts, "There is a message from Bravo Team, and they have landed on the top of the hill and are moving to engage. We can catch these guys in a cross fire and decimate them."

Mac and Chief Carison use a slight bend in the road and the tall grass to cross the road without being seen. On the other side, Mac motions for Carison to move up a few feet in the brush while he stayed on the road. Both men advance toward the UN Soldiers. Mac turns to Carison and points his trigger and middle fingers at his eyes then toward the soldiers. They move forward slowly picking off the enemy targets as they advance. Mac's

Stoner unleashes a maelstrom on the UN Soldiers. Chief Carison's M-4 rips through targets of opportunity. The UN Soldiers are caught unaware.

* * * * * * * * * * * * * * *

MC Myers and the rest of the team see the incoming fire has neutralized the UN Force to half of what it was. They break cover and advance up the hill.

"Bravo, this is Alpha, we are engaging from below." says MC Myers.

"Alpha, Bravo copies." says Lt. Block.

"Chief, Lt., we will meet you in the middle," advises Carison.

* * * * * * * * * * * * * * *

The UN Soldiers are taking fire from three sides, and are taking heavy casualties; the order is given to surrender. The UN Soldiers lay down their weapons and hold their hands in the air. The SEAL Team stops firing and start giving commands to the men.

The SEAL Team stands guard after rounding up the remaining UN Soldiers. Ensign

Mallow and Mitchell are treating the wounded as best they can with their limited resources.

Mac, John, Tony, Lt. Block, Chief Carison and MC Myers approach the confiscated Russian helicopter. Hands are extended, pats on the backs. Tim, who has been monitoring the radio, walks towards the men, "The fleets helicopters should be here any time. They were staged just across the border awaiting orders. Once they have landed, I'm to take our boys to Ramstein. The rest of the team is already en route."

****

As the helicopters are landing, troops move into position, Mac gathers up his men and the SEAL Team, "I know this doesn't have to be said, but I'm going to do it anyway. Thank you!"

MC Myers puts his hand on Mac's shoulder, "You would have done the same for us if the shoe was on the other foot. And you shouldn't have been there in the first place. If the government would have let us do the job we are trained for."

Mac shakes the hand of each man, and when he gets to Chief Carison he puts his arm around him, "I'm proud of you. More than you will ever know. Come home soon, spend some time with us."

"I will, Dad, soon as I can get some leave scheduled."

"See to it that Shane!" adds Mac.

"I'll do my best." Says MC Myers

* * * * * * * * * * * * * * *

Mac, John, Tony and Tim board the helicopter, the rotors spin up and they leave the ground. The men start interrogating the radio operator. The helicopter fades into the distance.

* * * * * * * * * * * * * * *

Sandy is standing in the kitchen making dinner and having a glass of red wine. In the living room the TV is on with FOX News running. The news caster "We here at Fox News wish to correct a story run by another network. It was previously reported that a group of Americans in Georgia that had previously been classified as terrorists are just the opposite. Through documents and images sent to us, we have been able to verify they did not attack a UN compound or execute any civilians. In reality they were attempting to protect and rescue those civilians. A joint Georgian, UN and US Military operation has stopped a rouge group of Russian soldiers that had infiltrated UN forces. Those civilians have been safely returned to their home countries. In other News…" Sandy smiles and holds her glass up as in a toast, "You really do help people." Says Sandy.

CHAPTER 14

Homecoming

The helicopter lands at an Air Force Base, as the men exit the helicopter, they are met by Don and two members of the Air Force's, Security Forces. The two Security Forces take custody of the radio operator. Greetings are exchanged.

"We can talk inside." says Don as he leads them to the rest of the team. They have entered a barracks where the rest of the team and the others are located. As the all come together they shake hands, hugs and thanks.

As Mac and Don move away from everyone, Dr. Anna watches them.

"So I don't see Dennis or Steve?" says Mac. Don's head is down, "Steve and Dennis were providing cover and were headed to the Osprey when they took a rocket hit. We got them both back to the Osprey, Steve and Dennis were in bad shape. Dennis took shrapnel to his back, probably won't walk again. He was medivacked here for additional surgery, and we are waiting to hear about his status. Steve, he died on the table."

Dr. Anna is still watching as Mac turns away from Don, he tries to raise his arms above his head but struggles and lets his arms fall back to his side. Mac walks to the wall and leans his head and arms against it. Dr. Anna walks over to Mac and touches him on the back, "I can't fix the hurting, but I can help with the pain, let me have a look at your injuries."

Mac turns to her and smiles, or maybe it's a grimace.

Mac takes his shirt off, and Dr. Anna is checks his injuries. Mac has multiple contusions, and a bullet wound on his left upper arm that is already healing. Dr. Anna begins to wrap Mac's ribs with bandages. Dr. Anna looks as if she wants to ask Mac a question, but doesn't.

****

Later that evening, Mac is awakened by one of the members of the base Security Forces, "My apologies for waking you but we have an inbound C-130 with the bodies of the fallen SEAL Team members. I thought you should know."

"Thank you, Chief Master Sergeant, we will be there to meet them and give them the proper reception."

Mac jumps from his bed, and rushes to wake the rest of the team.

Mac and the rest of the team dig through the gear they were given when they arrived at the air base and find new multicam uniforms. They quickly dress and meet on the flight line just in time for the arrival of the C-130.

Dr. Anna and the other two doctors, awakened by the commotion, follow Mac and the others on tarmac. They stand off in the distance and watch as the C-130 comes to a rest, the back loading gate begins to lower. The group of men all come to attention and salute as five flag-draped coffins exit the cargo bay escorted by two men, both in Navy Dress Blues, a tear rolls down Dr. Anna's cheek as she watches.

Master Chief Myers and Chief Carison escort their fallen brothers in arms into the hanger, the others follow. Once in the hanger, Mac and the others meet with MC Myers and Chief Carison.

"We are here to refuel and pick you all up before we head to Andrews. We will stand guard over our brothers till we re-board the C-130." says MC Myers. The men stand on either side of the five coffins at attention, while the others head off to gather their gear. Mac turns around to speak to his son, "We can talk on the flight back to the states." says Chief Carison. Mac nods his head in acknowledgement.

It doesn't take the men long to gather up their gear and board the C-130. The doctors first, followed by the team, then the coffins and finally MC Myers and Chief Carison. The rear gate closes and the C-130 taxi's to the runway where it lifts off into blue skies.

* * * * * * * * * * * * * * *

The plane had been airborne for a couple of hours when Dr. Anna approaches Mac, who has been talking to his son since the plane took off. She stands there for a couple of minutes, not knowing exactly how to interrupt them, when John walks up and kicks Mac in the leg, "Oh, excuse me, Mac, didn't realize you were talking." John smiles at Dr. Anna.

"Do you have a minute, there was something I wanted to ask you last night, but I, I wasn't sure how to. So, can I ask you a question?" says Dr. Anna as she sits down next to Mac.

"Sure, I'm sorry I didn't notice, we haven't had much time together." says Mac.

"How did you end up here?"

Mac looks around to see that Dr. Anna's question has drawn the attention of everyone.

"Well, this will be good practice since I'm gonna have to have this talk again soon. So, I'll try to give you the Cliff Note's version."

"I had only been there a month and was working the Marine Embassy detail in Lebanon, October 23,1983, the day the barracks was blown up. I wasn't in the barracks, but I was on my way there when the blast took me off my feet and knocked me out. When I came to, I rushed to the aid of my brothers. We did what we could, but it wasn't enough, we lost two hundred forty-one souls that day; two hundred twenty Marines, eighteen sailors and three soldiers.

They had a pretty good idea who had done it, so two days later, ten of us were sent on a mission to find those responsible. We found the guy we were looking for, but a number of years later I found out our Commanders sent us into an ambush in order to bolster a CIA deep cover operative. We sure pissed off a lot of people that day. When the fire fight was done we had killed forty-three attackers in all, and I believe their CIA operative, but they had killed eight of us.

"Sgt. Brooks and I were injured pretty bad, but we managed to keep our prisoner safe and get him out. The prisoner provided the name, Imad Mughniyah." Mac's mind returns to those days long past as he recalls the mission. Mac looks to Dr. Anna, tears in his eyes, "It took twenty-five years, but we got the bastard."

I spent two months healing and in physical therapy before I went back to being an MP and was on active duty with them for three years. In 1987 I requested and went to the Marine Special Operations School and spent three years. That's where I found out the Marine Corps sent us out to die that day in Lebanon and I chose medical retirement in

1990. Since my skill set was limited, I did the next closest thing. I was a Police Officer, and felt like I was making a difference. Everything seemed to fall in place. I was in negotiations with CPS and I even thought I had a job with the Secret Service, but when they asked if I'd take a bullet for Clinton, I hesitated a second or two and said where would I get shot? They didn't have a sense of humor.

Then we got a new Police Chief Joe Kaley, and that's when everything seemed to change. I lost my faith in the system. I will never forget that name, Kaley, I was more worried about the criminals I worked for, than the criminals on the street. No one would do anything about it. So I took all the skills I had learned and what fifteen years later here I am. It's more detailed than that, but that is it in a nut shell."

"I'm, we, are glad you do what you do." Dr. Anna leans up and kisses Mac on the cheek then walks away.

Mac smiles, "And that's why I would consider staying on."

Tim walks up to Mac and the rest of the team puts his hand on Mac's and Don's shoulders, "You guys are the best. I would fly into a hot LZ anytime for you. I'm proud to be a part of this team." He hand Mac his letter back and he starts to walk away, he begins sniffling...then laughing. The rest of the team is laughing and joking around giving each other a hard time.

Don stands up, and pats Mac on the back, "Our teammate said it so eloquently in his story, but the truth be told, Dr. Anna, we all do it for more than the money, or the glory." Everyone laughs at that one. "And we don't do it for, the adrenalin rush we do it for the heartfelt thanks from you and the hundreds of others like you. The look in their eyes when they are returned to their loved ones. That is why we do what we do. Anyone of us would give our lives or trade places with those five brave souls in a blink of an eye. Because we believe in our freedom and what we do to keep that freedom.
Our plane will land soon and we have to go our separate paths. You have to remember your promise, that we were never here, we did not rescue you. It was a joint United Nation and SEAL Team operation. Without your help, when the next person needs our help we may not be

able. You are as much a part of us now as we are a part of you."

Dr. Anna takes Don's hand, "You have our promise, our oath to protect what you do." The other two doctors take the hands of the team members. Hugs and thanks are shared all around.

* * * * * * * * * * * * * * *

The C-130 taxis to a secluded hanger. Once the C-130 stops outside of the hanger the rear hatch opens, and the doctors are met by Air Force personnel who escort them to an awaiting vehicle. The rest of the team and the CIA personnel begin to exit the aircraft. They form two lines on either side of the ramp and stand at attention as Master Chief Myers exits followed by the five caskets, then by Chief Carison. Dr. Anna stops the driver of the vehicle and the three doctors get out of their vehicle and stand and watch the procession. Once they have entered the hanger the doctors get back into the vehicle and drive away.

Inside the hanger, Air Force personnel take possession of the caskets. A Lt. Colonel approaches the Master Chief. MC Myers salutes and the Lt. Colonel returns the salute. Then he extends his hand, "We will take good care of your men Master Chief, they will be treated with the utmost respect."

"My thanks, Sir. I know they will." The Lt. Colonel turns away and joins the Airmen.

MC Myers, Chief Carison and Mac shake hands.

"Thanks for brining my boy home even if just for a short time." says Mac.

"It's the least I could do for an old friend."

"We have a couple of day's duty here on Funeral Detail, before I can come to St. Louis." states Chief Carison.

Mac smiles, "Take care of your men, Woofies will still be there."

Mac and his son embrace. Then MC Myers and Chief Carison head toward the caskets, "Woofies?" asks MC Myers. "Yep. The best damn hotdogs in the civilized world." Chief Carison turns around and hollers at Mac, "You're buying old man!"

****

Mac joins the rest of the team near the private jet waiting on them.

"Well boys, the company jet will get you home. With Dennis recovering, I have some team leader debriefings to do. Also, Dennis will be taking Smith place as he was promoted." says Don.

Mac stops Don, "If you would let CPS know, and I'm going to let Sandy know that with Dennis sitting behind the desk I'm going to stay on. Have them send over my new contract and any assignments they might have in mind." Don shakes Mac's hand "I'm glad you're the one that's going to tell her!" Laughs Don. "And I'm really happy you are sticking around; with Dennis most likely desk bound they are going to be relying on you and your experience even more now." Says Don.

"To be honest that's the only reason I'm going to stay. I trust Dennis, and I know he would never allow what just happened to us to ever happen. I trust you guys with my life." Says Mac. Don puts his hand on Mac's shoulder, "Having that trust is why we put our lives on the line. We know we will be there for each other no matter what."

The men all shake Don's hand, load their gear and board the aircraft.

* * * * * * * * * * * * * * * *

Mac drives up the road in his Dodge Challenger and pulls into the driveway. He grabs his gear and walks to the front door. Mac sets down a bag and opens the screen door, then pushes the door bell. He waits. A couple of moments later the door opens and there stands Sandy. Her eyes open wide and fill with tears.

"So can I come in? I have a lot to tell you." says Mac.

Sandy jumps into Mac's arms, she is holding on tight to Mac, her arms and legs wrapped around him. She hugs and kisses Mac as he carries her and his gear inside the house.

Once inside Sandy pushes on the front door and it closes. The TV is on Fox News, but no one is paying any attention. Mac drops his bags and walks off with Sandy in his arms.

Fox News is airing a special newscast on what had originally been believed to be an earthquake in North Korea. But Fox reports that it has been confirmed by North Korea that they have successfully tested a Nuclear Warhead underground.

A couple of moments later Mac walks back into the room and stands in front of the TV, Sandy follows Mac.

"Son of a Bitch!" exclaims Mac.

Sandy puts her arms around Mac.

"I'm guessing you're going to be getting another phone call late one night very soon?"

"Not right way, and it won't be for that anyway." Mac turns into Sandy's arms and looks her in the eyes.

"A lot has happened in the last few days, I'm not questioning what I do anymore. I know what I do helps people, I know that if I make a difference for just one person that everything, the sacrifices I make, we make is all worth it." States Mac. Sandy puts her fingers over Mac's lips. "Whatever you decide you want to do I am in it with you." Mac smiles at her. "So when the call comes and it will come, I will answer it. But let's just enjoy the time we have right now."

****

Break Contact is a work of fiction. All names, places and events mentioned in this book are the product of the author's imagination. Any resemblance to living person's and locations is coincidental.

Author's Notes:

Background Information

The idea for this story came from my experiences, activities, thoughts, ideas and information from friends. I combined all that material and filled in the gaps with my own imagination to create the finished story. I am fortunate to have a couple of close friends who were able to collaborate, and help guide me. A special thanks to Stewart and Shane for their input and a special thanks to Dan and Mike for their hundreds of hours of proofreading and editing.

From the Author

Over the past three years, I have spent countless hours writing, rewriting and collaborating on the ideas which have flowed through my head. I hope you enjoy reading. The people and events portrayed in the pages of this novel are fictional. "Break Contact" is a project that required me to do extensive research and draws on much of my own knowledge and life experiences. If you are reading this novel, you hold in your hands the result of more than three years of work. I want to thank you for taking your time to read my work, and I hope you enjoy the story!

www.ingramcontent.com/pod-product-compliance
Lightning Source LLC
Chambersburg PA
CBHW051455170626
46811CB00002B/499